You know how it is. You pick up a book, flip to the dedication, and find that, once again, the author has dedicated a book to someone else and not to you

Not this time.

This one's for you.

MICHEL F. BOLLE

HEY JULIE

A WHOLE LOTTA TOUCHING LOVE STORIES…

Cover : Michel F. Bolle
Artwork : Michel F. Bolle
Pictures : https://www.pixabay.com/

Publisher: Michel F. Bolle Publishing

ISBN
Paperback 9798371573544

About the author

Michel is undoubtedly a very special person. When you meet the imposing two-meter man for the first time, as I did in 2007 during a leadership symposium in Zurich, one could almost get involved with fear. But it does not take long until you feel and see that you are dealing here with a warm-hearted and very down-to-earth Swiss Guy.

Michel has this rare ability to tackle everything he tackles with incredible passion and immediately inspire people around him for his projects.

Over the many years of our friendship, I was fortunate enough to get to know his various facets and talents. As a volleyball coach, businessman, Leadership expert, friend and in privileged moments also as card magician.

No matter what role he is in, two constants are always the same. Michel is a unique storyteller, and he has an unmistakable sarcastic humor. Not infrequently, our dinners did not end until the early hours of the morning, after entertaining the whole restaurant with his fascinating stories or card and mental tricks.

He always stands firmly on the ground with both feet and has always remained true to himself, despite his success and the media hype. A charisma that makes a special difference to Michel.

"I have crafted most of the following love stories from 2020-2022 in a magic hostel called: Le Chateau *de Quesmy. A truly amazingly inspirational place"*

Michel F, Bolle

The Swiss Hostel

Nicolette closed her book and sighed. She had just finished reading the most beautiful love story…now what was she supposed to do?

She had only been home for a week, and she'd read three books from cover to cover. That was probably more than she'd read over the entire school year. It wasn't that she loved reading so much, there just wasn't much else to do on her parents' farm.

She began to wonder how she was going to keep herself busy for the entire three months of summer before she headed back to school in the city. The city, where there was always a museum to explore, a play to watch, or a movie to go see.

It was beautiful here, with breathtaking views of the Alps everywhere you looked, a pasture where the goats and sheep grazed all day, and a lovely little babbling brook next to a shady oak tree, but she found herself bored most of the time.

She could appreciate though that it was an idyllic location, and her father hoped that tourists would feel the same way. He had just transformed the old barn into a hostel for backpackers that wanted to experience "the simple country life."

Nicolette threw her long brown hair over her shoulder and stretched out on her blanket. She stared up at the snow-capped mountains towering above her, daydreaming about reaching the top and seeing what was on the other side.

"Hi, do you have rooms available?"

Nicolette snapped out of her reverie and turned around. A boy with sandy-colored hair and blue eyes about her age stood with a small group of two other guys and a girl with huge packs strapped to their backs. They were standing in the yard, five feet from where she laid out on her blanket. She scrambled to her feet.

The girl stepped up to the front of the pack. "Look, do you have rooms or not? The website said you had availability." She held up her phone in front of Nicolette's face. Nicolette could already tell she was not going to like this group. But she wanted to help her father get his business going, and if they left a bad review because the staff was rude, it would not be good.

"Yes, right this way. How many rooms will you be needing? Or we have separate male and female dormitory rooms for a discounted price if you'd prefer that."

"The dorms will be fine," the boy with the blue eyes said, smiling at Nicolette.

She guided them into the barn and stepped behind the small check-in desk. "If you can all sign your name in this book here. I'll show you to the dorms."

After Nicolette had shown them to their rooms and made sure they had everything they needed, she let them know that dinner would be served at 7:00, and they were free to explore the farm as they pleased.

"Will you need help cooking?" The blue-eyed boy came up to her and smiled. Her stomach did a little flip flop.

"If you would like to help, that would be wonderful! My parents will do the cooking, but I could use some help gathering the ingredients. I'm Nicolette." She held out her hand.

"I'm Trevor." He smiled and they shook hands. Her stomach did another flip flop.

"Well, aren't you friendly?" The blonde girl walked up to them. "So what is there to do around here?"

Nicolette smiled. She really did not like this girl. There are some good paths nearby for hiking."

The girl laughed. "A hike? I don't think so. I'm going to lay out and tan." She walked away.

Trevor turned to Nicolette. "Sorry about her. She would rather be laying on a beach on the French Riviera right now."

"Oh, well I can't imagine your girlfriend is going to have much fun around here, then."

"She's not my girlfriend." Trevor smiled at Nicolette again.

"Oh." Nicolette blushed and nervously tried to change the subject. "Well, would you like to come and pick some vegetables from the garden with me? We can use them for dinner tonight."

Trevor and Nicolette spent the afternoon pulling vegetables and getting to know each other. He told her all about his summer backpacking trip, and she told him all about her first year of studying in a new city, away from everything she'd known.

"It's hard to be away from home, isn't it?" Trevor asked her.

"It can be. But then when I'm home, I yearn to be out there again." She looked off in the distance.

"You could come with us."

"Wh-what?" She was caught off guard by his statement.

"Come with us. It would be nice to have a girl around who thinks about something other than her tanlines all day. And plus, I want you to come." He touched her arm, and she almost screamed 'Yes!' on the spot.

"I will think about it." She smiled and picked up the basket of vegetables. "Dinner should be ready in about an hour. I will tell you then."

Dinner was a casual and friendly affair. Everything was fresh and delicious, and not even the suntan girl could find any faults with the meal. After dinner, Trevor helped Nicolette clean up.

"Well, do you have an answer for me yet?"

Nicolette put down the dishes she was gathering. "I just don't think I can do it. My parents can use the help around here, and what will happen when you tire of me?"

Trevor stepped forward until he was directly in front of her. He reached up and tucked a loose strand of hair behind her ear. "I could never tire of you. Don't you want to see the world with me?"

"I do. But, I just can't." She hung her head and turned to go. He caught her hand as she walked away.

"We are leaving at sunrise tomorrow. I will be waiting under the oak tree for you." He pointed to the tree she had been lying under when they first met. "Meet me there if you change your mind." He squeezed her hand, then left to go back to the dormitory.

Nicolette laid in bed that night with her mind made up. She let out a deep breath, turned off her lamp, and fell asleep.

The next morning, the group had packed up all of their belongings and were ready to walk the short distance to the bus stop down the road.

"I'll meet you all there," Trevor called out to them as he stepped under the oak tree, anxiously waiting for any sign of movement coming from the main house. All the windows were completely dark, and he began to lose hope. He sighed and began to walk to the road.

"Aren't you forgetting something?"

Trevor stopped in his tracks and turned around. There was Nicolette appearing from behind the tree, a large pack strapped to her back.

"You're coming?" Trevor tore off his pack and ran to her.

"If there's still room for me." She looked up at him, smiling as he stepped closer to her.

"There will always be a space for you on my journey." And with that, he placed his lips upon hers, promising the beginning of a new adventure, together.

Swiss Chocolate and Swiss Cheese

Leon set down the tray of chocolate truffles and flipped the sign in the window from "Closed" to "Open." After being closed for a week while he went camping, he was happy to be back in his chocolate shop, doing what he loved.

He had been running the shop on his own going on six years now, and always looked forward to his customers' faces when they first stepped foot in the shop. The aroma would hit them first, then the sight, and then they would look to Leon for help. He had gotten to know exactly what his customers wanted the moment they walked through the door. Monsieur Müller would want chocolate-covered dates. And Madame Baumann always wants eclairs. And then there's the children that come here after school has ended that just want a chocolate bar to eat and spoil their dinner.

The shop was located in a small village where Leon had lived since he was a young boy. His father had been a chocolatier and had taught him everything there was to know about gourmet chocolate making. Everyone knew Leon in the town, and he knew them.

"Good morning, Madame, will it be another box of truffles for you today? We have some exciting new flavors to try!" The woman who ran the tailoring shop a few doors down had just walked in. She was notorious for grabbing a box of truffles on the way to open her shop almost every day.

"Hello, Leon! Yes, let's take a look at those new flavors…chocolate orange, chocolate raspberry, oh my! Chocolate blueberry! Yes, I'll take all of those, and give me two of the mint ones as well, and the peanut butter. Isn't it a beautiful day today? A perfect day for your new neighbor to move onto the lane!"

Leon was reaching for the chocolate peanut butter truffle when he stopped and looked up. "A new neighbor?"

"Yes! A woman. She took the old shoe store straight across from you. I am surprised you did not see it. But I forgot, you have been gone for a week."

Leon finished packing up the box and handed it to the woman, then walked over to the window. Sure enough, the windows across the lane had been washed and covered with paper. A sign on the door between the windows read "Sophia's Cheese Shop: Opening Soon!"

"Sophia?" Leon thought about everyone he knew in the town. "I do not think I know a Sophia. Is she from the village? Surely, I would have heard of her plans before I left for my camping holiday."

"That's just it…she isn't from the village! No one knows where she is from exactly, but then again, no one has talked to her! I did see her walking down the lane early this morning…she is very young and beautiful. I don't know how she is opening a shop for cheese all on her own, unless someone left her some money…oh well, I guess we will find out in due time! Thank you, Leon, and I shall see you tomorrow."

And with that, she closed the door and left Leon alone in the shop again. He looked across the lane and thought he caught a flash of movement behind the papered window. Perhaps he should go over there and knock on the door to say hello. The door to his shop opened and two women stepped inside. I'll go over there after I close this evening, he thought.

Leon grabbed his coat and flipped the window sign from "Open" to "Closed." He turned off the lights and stepped outside. The sun was just starting to go down as the dusk settled in. The streetlamps in the lane flickered to life as he took the few steps over to the new shop and gently but firmly rapped his knuckles on the covered glass door. A scraping sound was coming from within that stopped abruptly when he knocked. He could hear footsteps approaching, and then the door opened.

The woman standing in the doorframe was covered in white dust from head to toe. She was wearing a pair of old overalls with patches of paint all over them, and a bandana around her head that kept her hair hidden.

"Can I help you?" She spoke to Leon in a rushed sort of way, as if she was very busy and needed to get back to something immediately.

"Uh, hi, I own the shop across the lane here. I was just coming to introduce myself. I'm Leon." Leon held out her hand but began to pull it away when he saw hers was covered in the same white dust that covered her whole body.

"Sorry, you've caught me at a bad time. I am scraping all the old paint off the walls in here, and there are layers and layers to go. Maybe you can come back another time?" And with that, she closed the door.

Leon couldn't believe the rudeness of the woman. Well, that's the last time I reach out and be neighborly to her, he thought to himself. He turned around and walked the two blocks home to his apartment, just as the sun had completely gone down, and nighttime had arrived.

He unlocked his door and stepped inside his apartment, just as his cat came to greet him and to let him know it was dinner time. Leon walked into the kitchen and pulled out a can of cat food. After he fed the cat, he poured himself a glass of wine and went to sit in his chair next to the window.

He took a sip and sat back, looking out the window onto the tiny village below, and thought of Katrina. His ex-girlfriend had moved out of their apartment a month ago, but he still couldn't stop thinking about her. She had wanted to move away and go to the city, but Leon wanted to stay here. So, she packed up and left her cat with him. The stars twinkled in the sky as he could hear the church bells start to ring. He was happy to stay in his village, with his chocolate shop, and could easily do so for the rest of his life. He knew it was time to start getting over her, but he wasn't sure how; he needed a distraction.

"Thank you Monsieur, and let me know if your wife doesn't like them. We can try something else next time." As Leon finished up with his customer, the door opened.

"I will be right with you." The phone had begun to ring and Leon went to answer it. As he was taking an order for a chocolate birthday cake on the phone, he looked over at the person who had walked in and his eyes widened. She had to be the most beautiful woman he had ever seen in his life. She had dark brown hair, the color of his richest dark chocolate truffles, and dark brown eyes to match. She moved about the store in a fluid motion, as if she glided instead of walked. Leon could not take his eyes off her.

"Ok, Madame, n-next Tuesday? At 12:00 for pickup? Ok. Ok. Thank you." He hung up the phone and took a deep breath. Maybe this was the distraction he was looking for. He walked up to the woman and greeted her.

"Hello, I'm Leon, this is my chocolate shop. Are you looking for anything in particular?"

She looked at him strangely. "No, I was just coming over since I had a minute. We met yesterday, remember?"

Leon looked confused until, suddenly, realization dawned upon him. It was the rude cheese shop owner. "Oh, hello." His entire demeanor changed, and he didn't feel like being as cordial to her.

"Hi, sorry I didn't tell you my name yesterday. I'm Sophia." She held out her hand and he shook it reluctantly.

"This is a nice shop you have here. Do people in this village really like chocolate that much?" She said, walking around.

"More than they like cheese, I imagine. I do very good business here."

"Well, maybe they don't know what they've been missing. This tiny little village is sorely lacking in variety."

He was becoming more and more annoyed with her, and was ready for her to leave. She may be breathtakingly beautiful, but he didn't need someone around who talked badly about his village.

"Yes, well, I've got some things to do in the back, so, if you don't mind…"

"Right. Well, I guess I'll see you around. After all, we are right across from each other." She smiled and opened the door.

"Yes. Goodbye." He scowled at her as he watched her cross the lane and walk back into her shop. She had taken the paper off the windows and Leon could see she had done a fair amount of work to the place. She'll just be a novelty. She'll never last here, he thought.

A week later, and she had a line that reached all the way down the lane coming out of her shop. Leon watched from inside his shop at her customers, eager to buy her expensive gourmet cheeses. He shook his head and looked around at his own store: completely empty. He had no idea that there could be so many cheese lovers in this village, especially ones that had been chocolate lovers previously.

He was locking the door to his shop just as she was stepping outside and closing her door. She smiled and looked at him. He looked at her with no expression on her face, then turned to walk in the direction of his apartment.

"Wait! I feel as if we got off on the wrong foot," Sophia had caught up to his pace. "Can I buy you a drink?" She looked up at him hopefully.

He stopped and thought about it. There was really no reason to hold a grudge against her, and it had been so long since anyone had asked him to have a drink with them.

"Alright. Let's go have a drink. There's a tavern on the other street, this way." Leon nudged his head to the right and they walked the short distance to the bar.

"So, why did you want to set up a cheese shop in a small village like this one?" Leon took a sip of his red wine and looked at her from across the table.

"Well, I grew up in the city, and I visited this village as a little girl with my family. I'd always loved it here, the simplicity, the peacefulness…it was a place I could see myself settling down in. And I remember visiting a fine chocolate shop where a very tall man with a beard sat behind the counter."

Leon smiled and his chest started to feel warm. "That was my father. It was his chocolate shop, and I took it over when he passed away several years ago."

She reached out and took his hand. "I am so sorry to hear that. From what I remember, he was a very kind man."

Leon looked down at her hand upon his. The warmth that started in his chest had spread to his whole body. Maybe she was the distraction he needed after all.

Several hours and a few drinks later, they left the tavern laughing.

"Where do you live? May I walk you home?" Leon asked Sophia.

"It's just around the corner. But yes, you can walk me home." As they walked, she slipped her hand into his. "It's cold tonight, don't you think?"

Leon stopped and took off his jacket. "Here, let me put this on you." He draped the jacket around her shoulders, drawing them closer together.

She leaned into him. "I feel better already." Her head tilted upwards, and Leon knew there was only one thing to do; he bent his head downward and kissed her.

Six Months Later…

"Is it time yet?" Sophia peaked out the window at the crowd that was gathering right outside. "Can we open the door now?"

Leon stood behind the counter smiling at her. "If you think it's time, my love, then it's time."

Sophia flashed him a smile that made his heart skip a beat, and she threw open the door.

"Welcome to The Gourmet Cheese and Chocolate Shop. We are only allowing five customers at once in the store at this time. Please form a line, and if the first five can come in, thank you."

Sophia ushered five customers into the doors, and they enthusiastically began to look around. Sophia walked up to the counter where Leon stood. "Do you see? We are a success already!"

"It is all you, my dear. You are the success." Leon picked up her left hand and kissed it, the diamond ring on her finger sparkling in the overhead light.

The End

Oh Julie

"Alright class, that's it for the day. Remember to study for the test tomorrow and have a good evening."

The teacher erased the chalkboard as the students began to gather their books.

"Julie? Julie!" Julie's friend Bernice was shaking her arm to try and get her attention.

Julie had been looking out the window when she was snapped out of her reverie. "What is it? Oh, it's time...It's time!"

Julie hurriedly packed up her school bag and waved goodbye to Bernice. She practically ran down the hallway and out the double doors onto the busy sidewalk. "It's time, it's time! Today's the day!" She said to herself as she happily skipped down the sidewalk. The record store was only a few blocks away from her school, and the coins she had been saving for weeks jingled merrily in her pocket. She was finally able to afford to buy the new album by her favorite singer in the world, none other than Shakin'!

She only hoped they still had copies of the album available. It had come out two weeks ago, and most of her friends had already gotten their copies. She checked the store yesterday and saw they had three copies left, but that was yesterday. She didn't know what could happen to them in 24 hours. She rounded the corner and saw the big red flashing sign that spelled out RECORDS at the end of the street.

The little bell over the door rang as she stepped inside. There were only a few customers and it didn't look like any of them had the Shakin' album in their hands, which gave her hope. She walked past the rows and rows of music genres until she came to the display stand for new music. She knew just what she was looking for; she flipped through the alphabetical names…O..P..Q…R…S..S..S…T. Wait..where was it! S, it should be right here! She flipped through all the S names again, and still didn't see it. Despair filled her as she looked around and tried to see if the album would magically appear somewhere.

"Are you looking for Shakin' again?" A salesclerk came up behind her and Julie whirled around, looking desperately at her. "You were in here yesterday, weren't you?"

"Yes I was! Please tell me you still have a copy left. I've been saving up my money for weeks now just so I could buy it today!"

"Well, it is a popular album…," the salesclerk replied. Julie's face fell and she felt as if she might cry.

"But you're in luck! We still have a few copies left, and we moved them over here to the rock section. Come, follow me and I'll show you." The sales clerk walked over to the front of the store and Julie followed dutifully behind.

She pulled the Shakin' album out of one of the stalls and handed it to Julie. "Is this what you're looking for?"

Julie gently took it from her hands and held it up. Instead of crying from sadness, now she felt like crying from happiness! She hugged the album closely to her and followed the sales clerk to the cash register. Once she had paid, she left the store and ran all the way home, not wanting to stop until she had reached her bedroom, and more importantly, her record player.

She reached her front door and threw it open, then took the steps to her room two at a time. "Julie? Is that you, dear?" Her mother called her from the kitchen.

"Yes, Mother! I'll be down later!" She went into her room and closed the door. She stopped for a moment to catch her breath, then took her new record out of its sleeve. She placed it carefully into the player, and set the needle down.

She laid down on the floor and listened to the beautiful sounds that were the music of Shakin'. She closed her eyes and imagined watching him sing in person, and catch her eye in the crowd. After being mesmerized and enchanted by Julie, he would sing every song that night just to her. Opening her eyes, she sighed. If only that could happen for real.

The next day, Julie walked into the courtyard at school and joined a group of friends that were sitting on a bench. One of them was playing a portable radio. "Julie, come listen to this!"

She leaned in closer to the radio. This weekend only in Zurich! Come and see Shakin' live in concert. Tickets go on sale starting at noon today and they'll go fast, so make sure you get yours before it's too late!

Julie couldn't believe her ears. Shakin'? Here, in Zurich? This weekend? It was a dream come true! She only hoped that her mother was listening to the same station…she knew how much Julie loved Shakin', and maybe, just maybe, she would buy the tickets for her. Julie did have a birthday coming up soon, and she wouldn't want anything else, except to see Shakin' in concert.

The rest of the school day went by painfully slow, and finally students were dismissed. Julie ran home to ask her mother if she bought the tickets, and when she reached her front door, she noticed a familiar looking red sports car parked on the lane…Aunt Alice was visiting!

Julie opened the door and searched the house. She couldn't find her mother or Aunt Alice anywhere. Just then, she heard two feminine voices coming from the garden...of course, they were outside! Julie ran to the back door and stepped outside. There was her mother and Aunt sitting at a table, having tea.

"Julie! Look at you, my my you have grown! Come and give me a kiss, dear." Julie walked over to her Aunt and kissed her on the cheek. "Aren't you becoming a lovely young woman! And you've gotten so tall since I last saw you."

"Hi Aunt Alice, I'm so happy to see you. Did you bring me anything?" Julie smiled at her and sat down at the table.

"Julie! That's very rude." Her mother scolded her. Aunt Alice laughed. "Oh my dear, you have not changed. I have brought something for you, in fact. Something I think you'll like very much. Now, come inside with me and let's go see what it is."

Julie looked at her mother who had a knowing smile on her face. "Go on, it's alright," her mother said. "It won't spoil your dinner."

Julie followed Alice inside and watched as her Aunt walked over to her pocketbook. She grabbed a white envelope from within, and handed it to Julie. "I believe this is for you, my dear. Think of it as an early birthday present."

Julie took the envelope from her Aunt's hands and opened it. What she pulled out was two tickets. She looked closer and read the name.

"Are these tickets for Shakin!?" Julie exclaimed and started jumping up and down. "We're going to see Shakin'!

"Yes, my dear! I know how much you enjoy his music, and so you and I will go see him this Friday night. Are you excited?"

Julie squealed and flung herself into her Aunt's arms. "I have never been so happy in my entire life!"

"Well, it gets better Julie. I talked to a friend of mine that works at the concert hall. We also have backstage passes. You are going to meet Shakin'!"

Julie was speechless. She was really going to meet Shakin'? This was a dream come true for her. She felt like the luckiest girl in Switzerland. No, the luckiest girl in the world! She had no idea how she was going to get through the rest of the week. She wasn't going to be able to focus on anything, only the fact that she was going to listen to Shakin' sing her favorite songs, and then she'd be able to tell him how much she loves him. She was going to remember this concert forever.

The next day at school, Julie couldn't wait to tell all of her friends the news.

"Oh my goodness, Julie! That is amazing!"

"Did you bring the ticket with you? Can I see it?"

"What are you going to wear? You have to look beautiful if you're going to meet Shakin'!"

All of her friends were crowded around her, asking her nonstop questions. Julie was so happy she thought she might burst.

"Alright class, please take your seats and open your books to chapter six." The teacher entered the room and Julie and her fan club took their seats. She opened the book to the assigned page, but Julie wasn't able to read the words on the page. She wouldn't be able to do much of anything that day; she was glad they had already taken their test yesterday. If it was today, she certainly would've failed it.

As she was leaving school that day, her mother and her aunt were waiting outside the school gate.

"I didn't know you were coming to get me!" Julie smiled and hugged her mother.

Her mother looked down at her. "I've decided since you're going to have a very special night, you're going to need a very special dress to wear. So, we are going shopping."

Julie beamed and hugged her mother even tighter. "I am the luckiest girl that ever lived."

"You certainly are," Aunt Alice said. "Now, what is your favorite color?"

"Red," Julie replied.

"Then we shall have to find the most perfect red dress for you to wear."

After they left their third dress shop with no success, Julie started to feel discouraged. "I guess I'll just have to wear one of my dresses I already have."

"Do not give up hope just yet," Aunt Alice said. I see a store there just up ahead that has some pretty dresses in the window, and we haven't been there yet. I think that place is going to be the one."

Julie looked weary. "If you say so."

They walked into the store and Julie's eyes were drawn to the back of the store immediately. They had dresses in every color lining the racks, and Julie felt herself pulled to the back by an unseen force.

"Do you see anything you like?" Her mother had joined her as Julie browsed through the racks of brightly-colored dresses. She saw yellow dresses, green dresses, blue dresses, but no red ones yet.

Just then, she heard Aunt Alice clear her throat behind her. Julie turned around and there it was...Aunt Alice was holding up the most perfect red dress she had ever laid her eyes upon. It was short, but not too short. It had ruffles, but not too many ruffles.

"Oh Mother, can I try it on?" Julie turned to her mother for permission.

"It's certainly a mature dress. Do you think you're ready to wear something like this, Julie?"

Julie nodded her head enthusiastically.

"Alright, take it into the changing room and try it on. Come out and show me when you're all finished."

Julie went into the room and lifted the dress up over her head. After she zipped it up, she stepped back and looked into the mirror. She looked beautiful, and no longer like the little 14-year-old girl she was. She walked out to the waiting area to show her mother and her aunt.

"Oh Julie, you look wonderful. I think this is the one." Her aunt walked around her in a circle and nodded her approval.

"What do you think, Mother? Will it do?" Julie looked at her for assurance.

"It's captivating on you, my love. Are you sure you want this one?" Her mother asked.

"Oh yes! No other dress will do!"

"Then this is the one. Now go and take it off so we can pay for it." Julie went over to kiss her mother on the cheek and skipped back into the changing room. She had found her perfect dress for her perfect night.

As she was leaving school on Friday, Julie felt as if she had wings, and could fly home. Waiting out the week had been torture, but now that her time had finally come, she almost wanted time to slow down. She wanted to savor every moment of this night, so she could remember it for the rest of her life.

She changed into her dress and walked down the stairs to where her Aunt was waiting. "Are you ready to rock?" Alice asked Julie.

"Absolutely!"

They arrived at the concert hall an hour before Shakin' was scheduled to go on. Julie and Alice squeezed their way through the crowds. "Can we go backstage now?" Julie asked her aunt.

"I don't see why not," Alice replied. They linked arms and headed to the side of the stage where a security guard stood. They showed him their backstage passes and he stood aside, allowing them to pass through. Julie's stomach was full of butterflies as she looked around her. People were running around left and right, and she had to make sure she looked where she was going, otherwise she might run into someone.

"Alice, you're here!" A man came up to Alice and kissed her cheeks. "Let me show you the way to Shakin's room. This is your niece, right? His #1 fan?"

Alice looked over at me. "This is her. Julie."

"Like the song! Shakin' will love that. Come, right this way."

Julie's heart was beating so fast, she could hardly believe she was seconds away from meeting the man she was completely in love with. She was almost afraid that she would faint at the sight of him.

His dressing room was full of people, and Julie couldn't see him anywhere. Her aunt's friend guided her to the back of the room, and there he was, sitting on a couch, wearing his jean jacket and looking drop dead gorgeous. All of a sudden, my feet became rooted to the spot where I stood, and I couldn't move forward.

"Shakin', this is your biggest fan, Julie. She's been dying to meet you," my aunt's friend said to him.

"Julie," Shakin' looked at her. "What a beautiful dress you're wearing. Come and sit with me."

Alice pushed the small of Julie's back forward and she began to walk. She sat down on the couch next to Shakin', unable to take her eyes off of him.

"H-hi. It's nice to meet you, finally." Julie managed to say. I just bought your new album this week and I've listened to it nonstop. I've wanted to see you in concert for the longest time, and now, this is better than anything I'd ever imagined." Julie started to shiver.

Shakin' looked at her and smiled. "But you're cold, here, take my jacket." He slipped off his jacket and handed it to her. Julie put it on, and hugged it to herself.

A woman with a clipboard came up to Shakin's side of the couch. "Shakin', you've got five minutes."

"Thank you." He turned back to Julie. "I hope you'll stay for the show. Tell you what, when I sing Oh, Julie tonight, I'll be singing it for you."

He stood up and smoothed his hair back. "And keep the jacket." He winked at her and joined the woman with the clipboard, who directed him out into the busy hallway.

Julie sat back on the couch and closed her eyes. Oh Julie, Oh Julie…Julie…Julie…

"Julie? Are you up there? Dinner is ready, come down and join us!"

Julie opened her eyes to the sound of her mother's voice. She looked around and saw that she was laying on the floor, in her bedroom. It was all a dream, she thought. I must have fallen asleep, and I dreamed of meeting Shakin'. Oh, if only it were real!

She stood up and left her room, sighing as she walked down the steps, and joined her parents for dinner.

The End

A Meeting on the Tram

The tram rolled into the next station and came to a stop. I looked out the window and saw the sky had started to darken, and clouds were rolling in. Luckily, I remembered to grab my umbrella today in my rush to leave the house. The rainy walk to the University of Zurich campus wouldn't leave me a soaking mess on the first day back to school. I could hear a voice come on over the loudspeaker and I took my headphones to listen better. Hopefully, there wouldn't be a delay; I was already cutting it close by taking the later tram today, leaving me only 15 minutes to travel the 10 blocks on foot to my school.

I put my headphones back in and sat back. I watched as a few people boarded the train…a businessman, a mother and her two children, and then, her. I leaned my head forward and sat up straight, so I could get a better glimpse of the girl that had just caught my eye. She looked my age, maybe 18 or 19, with long red hair that fell down her back. She had brilliant blue eyes, and lips so red there was never a reason for her to ever wear lipstick. She was petite but curvy, and had the most pleasing figure I'd ever seen. In fact, everything about her was pleasing. I'd never known someone I had just seen and hadn't even spoken to could make me feel such a strong reaction. I watched her as she moved down the aisle, looking for a place to sit.

When she saw there was an empty seat next to me, she gave me a look and smiled. I could feel that look in the pit of my stomach.

"Is this seat taken?" She asked, her voice sounding cheerful and melodic.

I shook my head, words escaping me at the moment.

She sat down and the tram began to move.

I kept trying to steal glances at her when I noticed she was doing the same thing with me. Finally, we both turned our heads at the same time and our eyes met. She smiled, and I smiled back at her, making me feel more relaxed.

"What are you listening to?" She pointed to my headphones.

"Oh, it's this podcast. The Science of Things. It's my favorite."

Her eyes widened. "What a coincedence!" She reached into her bag and pulled out her phone and showed it to me. "I listen to that show every week. Are you listening to their latest episode? I just finished it!"

"That's amazing! I've never met anyone that listens to them regularly. It's quite refreshing, actually. I'm Daniel." I held out my hand to her.

She laughed and shook my hand. “I’m Danielle.” Then we both laughed.

We had about 20 minutes left until I came to my stop, which was her stop as well. It turned out we attended the same university. We kept talking throughout the tram ride and realized we had almost everything in common, a realization that surprised both of us.

Just then, rain began to hit the windows. “Oh darn,” she said, as she looked outside. “I forgot my umbrella.”

“I have mine. Maybe we can share it and walk together?”

She smiled and reached for my hand. “I’d like that.”

The time had come, and our journey on the tram had come to an end. She stood up and walked into the aisle, while I followed behind. I handed her the umbrella since she was going to be the first one to step outside, and the rain was pouring down by now.

It seemed as if almost everyone on the tram was getting off, and it created a little traffic jam. She looked back at me and rolled her eyes. I smiled at her, happy that I had met someone I could joke around with and talk to so easily. Danielle put me at ease, and I couldn’t wait to get to know her better. I’d have to find out what her schedule was, and see if we could meet up for lunch. Then coffee. And then dinner. Then maybe we could go and catch a movie later. Judging from how she kept looking back at me and smiling, she most definitely had the same idea.

As she stepped off the train, there was a huge crowd. She reached back and grabbed my hand, the pouring rain on the open platform made it hard to see what was in front of me. As we continued to weave our way through the crowd, a sudden jostling of eager passengers making their way through to get onto the train broke the connection of our hands and I looked ahead for Danielle; she was nowhere to be seen.

I looked to the side, behind, and stood on my toes to see if I could glimpse a view of her vibrant red hair. I saw nothing but the black of everyone's umbrellas and the grayness of the rain coming down. I made my way over to the stairs that led down to the street. I turned around once more and looked…nothing. Realizing I was going to be late for my first class if I waited any longer, I begrudgingly went down the steps and walked the 10 blocks in the rain to school.

I had made it into the Chemistry lab room with a few minutes to spare. Soaked to the bone, I grabbed a tissue out of my bag and wiped my face off with it. I looked for somewhere to sit and found an empty table with two seats at the back of the room. I didn't really feel like talking to anyone after losing Danielle in the crowd, so I went and sat by myself. I couldn't believe that we had lost each other, and now I had no way of reaching her. I may never see her again.

"Is this seat taken?" I knew that cheerful, melodic voice. I looked up and there she was, looking as radiant as ever. I nodded and she sat down.

She held out my umbrella. "I think this belongs to you." I took it, my fingers brushing over hers.

"You're in this class?" I looked at her and couldn't believe my luck.

She nodded, then reached for my hand under the table. "I knew we'd find each other again. That's just what happens when people are meant to be together."

The End

ALPEROSE

… love where you least expect it!

Robert had many things running through his mind. If he clinched this deal with Mr. Ocean, he would finally have his revenge on his father-in-law and his own family who had alienated him.

Of recent, business deals were snatched under his nose by the Weinsteins. His suspicion rose after the third occurrence, but he decided to keep mute. He would beat them at their own game.

This current deal would be a close deal. No one would know about it. That was why he decided against flying to driving all the way up, to a beautiful and completely lost place in the Swiss Alps, to arrange a very special vacation for Mr. Ocean. He was currently returning to Zurich. To-night, he would sign the deal, and his revenge would be satisfied.

+++

Alice had never had a vacation in her thirty-five years. She had spent almost all her life moments in Kandersteg. She had always dreamt of a vacation, but she could not afford it. Therefore, when Kylie, her best friend, decided that they visit an amazing place in the Alps for girl's trip, Alice could not refuse.

The best part of the trip was that Alice would not get to pay a dime. She only needed to submit her time, humor, and car, then all would be set.

At the Alps, they had gone on a fall and trail running, they went caving, they did a downhill mountain bike ride, and they went kayaking. They had the fun of their lives over the course of three days at the Alps.

A day before they were to return, Kylie had an emergency. She booked a plane ticket and left that night. Alice would have to drive all the way back to Kandersteg the following day. It was going to be boring, but she was glad she had an album of Shakin' Stevens to keep her company.

+++

Robert and Alice did not know that they were about to be held ransom by destiny. Would it be a kidnap or a beautiful memory to remember? It was all in their hands to decide.

Chapter One

Robert was driving his black Bentley down from the Swiss Alps. Even though the ambient air was cold and there was a thunderstorm coming, he decided against sliding down the windows. Instead, he had switched on the artificial air conditioning of the car. It was blowing cold, and he loved it that way.

It was few minutes past four in the evening, and he was looking to get to Zurich on time. He had a client, Mr. Ocean, coming from Seattle in America and he would like to receive him personally at the airport. He could not imagine missing it for the world. This was a deal worth thirty-five million dollars. It would be the highest he has ever been involved in.

Robert wished he could accelerate more than he was currently doing, but he could not do that without hitting the Citroën 2CV ahead of him. Its driver looked like a woman.

Women and their unseriousness.

He could not overtake the car because the road was a single lane, so he turned on the headlight of his car and started flashing it. He had hoped the driver would catch the reflection of the blinking headlight in her rear-view mirror, but to his dismay, the driver did not behave as if she noticed anything. This made Robert change strategy.

He pressed his thumb on his car horn and pressed it several times that soon; the sound of the horn was like the beats to a pop song. Still, the car ahead did not increase its speed.

+++

Alice was driving her almost antique Citroën 2CV car down from the Swiss Alps, and she was at an average speed of 60km/hr. She had wound down her car window so that the cold mountain zephyr would blow inside. She had the music turned on at a high volume, and the mixture of Shakin'Stevens's sonorous voice and beats were filtering out of the car's four speakers.

Her phone vibrated in her pocket. She took it out. It was a message from Julian, her brother.

"When will you be home?"

Alice could not risk replying to the message while driving, so she tucked the phone back into her pocket.

She started a karaoke with the music, and she would periodically take her hands off the wheel and fling them to the gyration of the musical beats. She was really enjoying herself. Then she saw something that was blinking in her rear mirror. It was flashing headlight. This made her turn towards the rear windshield and checked whom it was. A young man dressed corporate with a stoic look. She guessed that he was one of those top shot bankers who lived in Zurich. He kept blinking his car's headlight.

What does he want?

She let her mind off it, and she continued to do karaoke to the Shakin'Stevens's *You Drive Me Crazy*. The blinking headlight had stopped. Then felt she heard something like a honk, so she reduced the volume of the in-car music player. The honks were sounding like the beats of a pop song.

Does he want me to go faster? If he likes, let him press the horn until eternity, I am not driving more quickly. If he is not satisfied, let him fly.

The death of her cousin, almost a year ago, on the same road, was what borne her stubbornness. He had gone racing with friends when he lost control of his steering wheel along a dangerous bend. The car somersaulted several times. When the rescue team got there, they could not remove the body as the car had wrecked grotesquely. They cremated the incomplete dismembered body parts the rescue team found.

+++

Robert did not know what else he could do. He really wanted to get to Zurich on time, but this car and its slow driver would never make it possible. A thought popped into his mind that he should speed up his car and ram the rear bumper of this old Citroën 2CV with it. Maybe it would make her stop the car and come out to make a confrontation. Then he could write her a check for the damages and tell her he has an emergency and he needs to speed up. It sounded nice in his mind, but Robert's smart counter-mind stimulated the idea and found that it could be equally dangerous as it was nice. He could ram his car into her. She could get a panic attack and lose control of her vehicle. An accident was likely to happen, and accidents on these parts would likely result in death. He would be charged to court for murder. If he were lucky, he would get life imprisonment, but his reputation would be ruined forever. Then he would sit up in his prison bed and wondered why he was not patient with the Citroën 2CV driver.

He decided against ramming her car. Instead, he would keep blinking the headlights and pressing the horn. He hoped it provokes a response.

+++

Alice hit her hands hard on the steering wheel.

Why do some men behave like animal?

She increased the volume of the music. The loudness made the honk sound like a whisper, but it ruined the beauty of the music to her ears. It was more like torture, so she reduced it.

She was trying hard to bottle her anger, but she was nowhere near succeeding. The man was now flashing his headlight and honking at the sometime. It was then she decided she has had enough. She gently applied the brakes, and the car came to a halt in the middle of the road. She flung the door open.

+++

Robert was happy when he noticed she was pressing brake. Now he would be able to tell her to speed up. His plan did work, after all, so he matched the brake pads too.

He opened the door as soon as the woman in Citroën 2CV car did and he went out, his shoes kissing the cold asphalt.

As he approached her, he could see the eyebrows on her heart-shaped face were furrowed and her hands balled. She was angry even though some of her auburn hair fell across her face. Her look did not disturb him, and he maintained a calm attitude. He had always faced angry customers all his life, and as he climbed up the career ladder, he had learned how to pacify even the lion-hearted ones.

'What exactly is your problem?" The woman spat at him as soon as he got close enough.

"Pardon my crazy attitude. I am in a hurry, and your pace is not good for me." He said in the softest of voice.

This was opposite of his nature, but he had learned that to pacify people, you must be able to admit errors that are not yours and treat your adversary like a boss. "I didn't get your name ma'am."

"I didn't throw it either." The woman said. The fury in her face was still there. "If you can't drive at my speed, then fly. People as rich as you are don't even drive nowadays."

"Well, I am not rich as I look—"

She cut him mid-sentence, "But you drive a Bentley. Keep your pretense to yourself. I am not one of those country ladies your sweep away with your charm."

"Trust me Ma'am; it is not what you think. I--"

The woman suddenly placed her hands on her lips and she hushed Robert shut. Robert was thinking she was rude until he noticed she was craning her neck to listen to something. Robert tried to listen too, but he could not hear anything peculiar from the normal ambient sound that had been on since he started driving.

"Run!" She shouted all of a sudden, pulling his arm and bolting off.

Robert was confused, but a jolt of adrenaline ensured he joined the rapid sprint. They raced back the road.

Chapter Two

Now he could hear the sound as he was running. It was an avalanche!

"That lane," the woman screamed, pointing to a lane that led into the forest. Without giving it any thought, he followed her into the lane.

After running for some minutes, Alice stopped when she felt they were at a safe distance from danger. She had heard the sound of a stone avalanche. Growing up in the mountainous village of Kandersteg, the sound of an avalanche (be it snow or stone) was not alien to her.

She was catching her breath when the young man arrived.

"You are one terrific runner," He said, catching his breath. "As fast as a bullet." He gestured with his folded fingers.

"Everyone is fast during danger. You weren't bad yourself."

"And still you arrived here several seconds before me."

"Well, let's say I do this pretty often.

Robert found a log at the edge of the lane, and he placed a leg on it. Alice chose to sit on the shrubs instead.

"Let's just take a few minutes and head back. I really need to be in Zurich." Robert said, taking his legs off the log and facing the small mountain road.

Alice did not respond. She did not even act as if she heard what he said.

Robert repeated himself. Still, Alice did not respond.

"I don't know why you young ladies are very rude." He moved closer to her. "I am telling you something, and you are not answering me."

Alice slapped her palms together. "You think I am one of those numerous ladies without dignity in the streets of Zurich? I should have left you to keep driving, and the avalanche should have rid the world of you. I am sure no one would miss such an ungrateful man like you."

"Oh, you wanted 'Thank you, ma'am, for saving my life," He curtsied while he talked. "Well, if not for your slow driving, I would have driven far, and the avalanche wouldn't have caught up with me. Now we should get going because it will soon be dark and we would be trapped here."

"Well, I am not holding you ransom. Go and drive the Bentley now turned rubble. That is if you even see it." She brought out her phone and started fiddling it with her thumb.

Robert was not going to have this nonsense. If the crazy woman wished, she could sit and spend the eternity there. He was not going to spend any more minute there. He better walked back to his car and drive to Zurich. Mr. Ocean would not be annoyed if he was late particularly when the news comes in that there was an avalanche. He stormed off through the path he had run a few minutes ago. Fury fed his legs, and he walked briskly. He could not imagine the audacity the crazy woman had to demand a 'thank you' because she pulled his hand and told him to run.

He was soon on the road, and he began to walk towards the spot where he had parked the Bentley.

"It is just after that bend," he muttered to himself, and then he began to jog.

By the time he came out of the bend, the sight before him was his wildest nightmare.

+++

Alice had not seen such an ungrateful man before. She was sure it was not because he came from Zurich. She had met many mountain hikers who come to Kandersteg from Zurich for holidays, and they were usually nice and kind. She knew he would return. Stone avalanche in these areas usually covered the roads and sometimes, it would take a week before the clear off the boulders and open the road for use.

Even though she would prefer to be on her own, she knew she was not equipped for the scenario she was in. She needed shelter, food, and clothing, and she was sure the rude man in some way could be helpful.

She knew he would be back, so she kept fiddling with her phone, checking the vacation pictures she took last with Kylie at the Alps.

+++

Robert could not believe it. Several boulders covered the road. Both cars were covered he could not see them. He could only imagine how wrecked his car must be under the boulder.

He really needed to get to Zurich before the plane landed.

A thought came into his mind. Why does he not try to climb the boulder to the other side? Maybe he would be able to hike a ride. Then he would come back for what is left of his Bentley. It seemed like an excellent idea, so he moved closer to the boulder and tried climbing. His fancy shoe was more deterring him than helping him, so he took them off, tied their laces together, and he hung them over his neck.

Climbing was now easier as he climbed a small boulder. The next boulder was so huge that there was nowhere to place his arm or feet to climb it. He tried to move to the left and then the right. The situation was the same thing. Dejected, he climbed back down.

Think Robert, Think.

How would he get across? All efforts to singlehandedly climb had been futile. He needed external help. There was no one around, except that mannerlessly girl who only cared about 'thank you.' He wished they had met in Zurich and she would know who he was.

There was no one around, and darkness was slowly taking over the skies. Soon, it would be dark. He would be without food and shelter. He did not think his suit could protect him against the cold of the Alps. If only he had his phone with him. He would have called his Mr. Barkley, and an emergency helicopter would be on its way to his location after they had triangulated where the call signal was coming from.

Maybe the crazy girl has a phone.

It came back to him. She has a phone. She was fiddling with it just before he left. He must get to her and somehow convince her to let him use her phone.

He set his shoes on the ground, untied the laces that were together, wore his shoes, and he was soon on the way to meet her.

+++

It would soon be dark. The battery on Alice's phone had turned to red, giving her a visual notification that it would soon be empty.

Where is this ungrateful man? He should be back already.

She had such a huge faith that he would be back. She had not seen the avalanche, but she was sure the intensity of the sound she heard was very loud. The road would be inaccessible, and their cars must have been wrecked. She was sure of it.

This was not the first time she would escape an avalanche. She had taken avalanche survival courses in the past, and she had learned the key to surviving an avalanche was a reaction. She had to run from the epicenter towards the side because avalanches are most dangerous in the middle where the bulk of the snow or stone are. That was why she grabbed the ungrateful man's hand and ran to the side.

Her phone screen flashed on 'battery low' followed by a warning tone. She turned it off to conserve the remaining battery. Restless for the moment, she decided to start to sing Shakin'Stevens's "Green Door".

+++

Robert had doubts if he was on the right path. There were two paths off the road, and he was not sure if it was the first they took or the second. He opted for the first and hoped that he was right.

When he heard a sonorous voice singing a song, he was sure he was on the right path.

The woman was still sitting on the grass, and she was singing. She was not fiddling with the phone as he expected.

"Hi." He relaxed his face and looked polite

The woman looked up, and she did not look surprised to see him. She stopped singing too.

"You forget something? Your car keys or what?"

Robert smiled. The woman was teasing him.

"I am sorry about how I treated you just before. You saved my life, and I should have been grateful."

The woman smiled. "Where did you hide this aspect of your character?"

"You must pardon me. I really acted unfairly." He stretched his palm. "My name is Robert Müller."

She stood and shook his hand, "Alice. Alice Frankhauser." She was now smiling. "One advice though. Never show that side of your character you showed me to anyone. No one deserves that character."

Robert set his gaze on her, still wearing the innocent look. He really needed her to believe he was sober for his action. Her phone was the only lifeline he had.

"I will try." Robert smiled again. "By the way, I saw you holding a phone the other time. Can I borrow it, please? I am sure you want to get out of here too."

Alice elongated the smile on her face. "So you can call your helicopter." She gave him the phone.

Robert collected it and pressed a button on the side of the phone. The phone screen did not light up.

"Oops. I switched it off to conserve the battery. Here let me switch it on." She collected the phone and switched it on, and then she returned it.

Robert collected the phone and inputted some numbers, and then he pressed the dial button but was shocked at the response.

No Network

"There is no network. Not even a single bar on the network strength bar."

"It's usually like that around these areas. We head better to the road. We might get a signal there.'

On Alice suggestion, she and Robert walked side by side towards the road. He kept staring at the signal strength on the way, but to his utmost dismay, the situation did not change.

Chapter Three

When they got to the small mountain road, the network situation still did not change, so Alice suggested they should climb to an elevated place. They were more likely to get better network reception there.

Robert remembered he saw a place among the mountain range just before the bend that looks like it something one could climb. He proposed that they went there.

It would be dark in about an hour, and Robert knew they must really find their bearing before then.

They got to the place Robert suggested, and it was something one could climb.

"Let me climb it," Alice offered. "I bet I am a better climber than you are."

"I don't think so," Robert replied.

Robert was already buckling off his shoes. "I got this." He tucked the phone into his pants pockets, and he started climbing.

The climb was tedious, but Robert did not show it. He kept bottling all the groans from the pains he felt as the sharp edges of the rock tore into his hands. After climbing some few meters off the ground, he was able to find a place to place both feet and make a call. He untucked the phone from his pocket.

"Did you get a signal?" Alice shouted from the ground.

Robert could see two bars on the signal strength.

"Yes. It is strong enough to make a call."

He pressed the number on the screen, and he dialed the number.

"It is ringing," Robert said excitedly.

Alice started dancing and the sight made Robert shake his head. "She is truly a crazy woman," he muttered in his head.

The call patched through.

"Hello, Mr. Barkley."

"Hello, Yes. Who am I speaking to?"

"Robert."

"I can't hear you, Sir. Could you repeat your name?"

"Robert."

'The network is terrible."

"Robert... Robert…Robert."

A warning tone overrode the call. Robert checked it.

Battery empty

Alice watched him from the ground. Robert was not talking on the phone again. Instead, he was staring at the phone screen.

"What's up?" She shouted.

Robert did not respond. Instead, he started climbing down the rock.

Alice was perplexed. Was Robert able to pass the message across? She doubted it. She heard every single word he said, and he was not able to say anything more than his name. On the other hand, maybe he sent a text message instead. She was thinking about it all when Robert descended off the mountainside and flashed her phone before her eyes.

"The battery is dead." His voice was dry.

Now she remembered the battery was low when she was fiddling with it, and it was the reason why she had switched it off in the first instance. That spelled doom but she needed to confirm it.

"Were you able to pass the message across?"

"No, the battery died before I could do so." He returned the phone to her.

This was what Alice had feared. Their chances of being rescued were now very low. They had better find shelter and house themselves until tomorrow.

"We had better find a shelter then."

"Maybe they would have a phone, and we call. I really need to get to Zurich."

"You have been saying Zurich since like I don't also have a home. What are you rushing there for anyway? Your wife is due for delivery?"

Robert furrowed his eyebrows when he heard 'wife.' "I don't have a wife. I have this client coming in from America, and it is important I meet him at the airport."

"So it is about money."

"Well, what isn't about money?"

"Your life for example."

"What's my life worth without the money in it?"

Alice was getting infuriated. Robert did not know what they were in. If he did, and then he would not place his client ahead of his survival.

"Well, money can't help the condition we are in now. We better quit talking and start looking for shelter. Soon it will be dark, and the cold would descend from the mountaintops. Frostbites would be riding our bodies by morning."

In as much as Robert hated it, Alice was saying some valuable nugget. He was already feeling the increased cold over the time they had spent been struck. He could not remember seeing a building for the past one hour he had been driving. If they should walk all the way back, he was not sure they would make it, and for the first time that evening, he felt fear.

Alice knew there would not be a settlement near. No one lives in these areas. However, they could be lucky to see a storage house or a chalet if they looked well enough.

"I am betting we go back the path we first ran to. I am sure it would lead somewhere."

"I was going to say that too because I can't remember seeing a house for the past one hour of driving."

They both retrace their steps to the path they had both left, and they kept walking down. It was a long path with knee-length shrubs and tall trees-the height of several story building, at the borders. The path was a frequented one. It was evident because it was bare and almost nothing grew there.

"You seemed happy walking down this path." Robert voiced his observation.

"And should I be sad?"

"That's not what I meant. Okay. Where do you live?"

"Kandersteg."

"Now I see how you were able to know the avalanche was coming. You are nature lovers."

"It's not because I come from Kandersteg or you come from Zurich. I know quite a lot of people who come to Kandersteg to climb mountains, and they are cool, you know-nature lovers. In the same vein, I know some people who live in Kandersteg, yet they hate anything that has to do with nature. Like my brother for instance."

"Well, I can't really say, it's just the—" the sight before him swallowed the rest of the sentence.

The path opened to a large field with an abundance of flowers. The skies were a picturesque dying orange, and there was no cloud in sight. On the horizon were peaked snow mountains. Even though he was not a nature lover, but this view kept him spellbound. To crown it all, there was a chalet about half a kilometer away.

'Look at that chalet." Robert announced, pointing to the small building in the distance.

Alice had already burst out of the path and was already in the midst of the flowers. She plucked one and perceived its fragrance. It smelt nice.

Robert was surprised to see Alice amidst the flowers, but he still needed to break his discovery to her. That made him go into the flower field, walking carefully so as avoid staining his pants.

‘There is a chalet over there. We should check it out.” Robert pointed his hand in the direction of the chalet.

Alice turned her head to where Robert was pointing. “I see it. But come and join me.” She plucked another flower and placed it under Robert’s nose. “It has a nice fragrance.”

Robert shrugged and took his nose away. “We should really get going.”

Alice did not feel like going anywhere. The fragrance of the flowers was everything she wanted. “You have three choices: either you join me, wait for me till I have my fill or you go to the chalet yourself.”

Robert did not say his decision as he started moving, apparently going for the third choice.

“One more thing,” Alice's voice rang out, “some of these flowers could be wild, and some could be carnivorous in nature. If I were you, I would wait.”

Robert would love to defile her words, but he knew he could not. Alice seemed like those who love and understand nature. He could not risk going headstrong and falling into prey of some wild plant, hereby knotting the problem at hand. He decided to wait until she was through.

He would have loved to sit down, but he could not find anywhere neat he could sit on. Though there was log at the mouth of the path where it opened to the field, he could not imagine himself sitting on it like those village dwellers.

He decided to stand and wait. With the chalet in sight, he was sure they had a place to stay in for the night. However, his focus was not to stay the night. He hoped they could find someone in the house and a telephone that works. He could tell Mr. Barkley to go and pick up his client and send a helicopter to him. His client, having heard his story would be likely glad for him and he might increase his bonus for the display of passion for working against all the odds.

It was sure the outcome would bc exciting if he got hold of a phone. Alice was still in the reverie she fell into by inhaling the flower. He stood and rechecked the chalet. He was looking for a sign of activity inside. He would be glad to see a movement or hear a sound from it. He looked, sending his gaze to the translucent window, but he could not see anything.

Meanwhile, Alice seemed to be through, and she was beckoning to him to come. "Shall we go now?"

"I thought you would sleep there?"

"I would have loved to, but I was considering you."

"You bet."

Alice led and they walk through the field. Robert was dusting his pants every now and then.

"The flowers. They won't stain your pants."

"How can I be so sure?"

"Well, I am used to them."

"How do I know you aren't deliberately lying to me as a punishment?"

Alice laughed. "And what might you have done wrong that I would decide to punish you."

"I don't know. Maybe because I refused to follow you into the field to smell the flowers."

Alice laughed again. "You are one funny man. You would make a good comedian, you know?"

"You think this is funny." His voice was harsh.

Alice stopped and looked back. "Do you even know how to take a joke?"

"No one jokes where I come from."

"So we that are living in Kandersteg are the comedians?"

"I didn't say that. You assumed."

"You can play around with words as you like, but I sure know you aren't the first person from Zurich I have met, and the ones I met are not ungrateful and killjoys like you are." She resumed walking.

Robert chuckled and he tapped his chest. "You mean I am a killjoy? You should see me when I play golf."

"I bet you don't play it because you love it. You probably went to play because your client loves it and you thought you would gain his confidence by playing against him and letting him win."

For the first time that evening, Robert was mad and impressed with her at the same time. She was right. He had no time to be swinging golf clubs at a white ball to fly over forest and lakes to enter a small hole. It is such a waste of pastime. Nevertheless, he could not help it when the business deal was going south, and he remembered Sheik Mansur once mentioned that he loved golf. He quickly recommended they went to play golf.

He was a very good player back in college, but he lost interest afterward when marriage came into his life picture. As soon as the game began with Sheik Mansur, Robert realized the Sheik was the kind who won games by switching ball positions with the help of loyal caddie. He had noticed that the caddie kept switching the position of the ball, but he did not want to voice out. It would counter the initial reason for playing the game. Even with all the help he could get, Sheik Mansur was still a bad shot. Robert deliberately shot awkwardly almost every time including missing a chance to win the game at a short range of 1.5 meters.

In the end, Sheik Mansur won the game and in his ecstatic mood, Robert brought up the business deal again. Within the next fifteen minutes, both parties reached an agreement.

Robert was so sure Alice would not know any of this, yet she sounded so confident like that FBI agent who profiled people by mere looking at them. Maybe she was a secret agent. Was she sent to watch him? Was Alice stopping her car in the middle of the road deliberate? Was the avalanche man-made to pair both of them together? Nevertheless, what could she be looking for? He did not have any shady deals that could worth investigation.

Alice was expecting a reply, but she heard none. When she swivelled, she was surprised to see Robert lost in thought. She stopped and snapped her finger so that Robert could see them and snap back to reality, but he did not. He kept on walking. Alice intentionally stayed on his path and Robert crashed into her.

Robert rammed on Alice and they both fell to the ground. He quickly got up and muttered, "Sorry," then he pulled her up from the ground and helped dust the dirt that clung to her jean trouser.

For the very first time in the day, he took a mental view of what of Alice's face. She had a heart-shaped face with few freckles on her fair skin complexion. Her hairs were cascading and they fell behind her shoulder. She was wearing a sleeveless white blouse with a pink floral pattern on it and blue jean trousers.

"I am sorry, I-" he lost the remaining sentence he wanted to say.

"Finish your statement."

"Are you a secret agent?"

Alice could not help but laugh aloud. "I have said it that you speak like a comedian. How can I be a secret agent? Everyone knows I own a small flour shop in Kandersteg."

Robert went silent. Maybe he had stringed impossibilities together when he suggested she was a secret agent. She had saved his life and even offered him his phone to make a call. He should be grateful. He really wanted to, but the contrasts of their character only made hatred possible.

"I am sorry I went too far with the FBI thingy. We better get back to the chalet business."

‘It’s nothing.” She picked up a flower she noticed was different to the majority on the field. “I just find it funny.” Then she resumed walking.

They did not say anything else until they got to the chalet.

The chalet was a small building made of brown wood with a heavy, gently sloping roof and wide, well-supported eaves set at the proper angles at the front of it. There was a flower planted in a clay bucket placed near the door. Around the chalet was a small wooden fence-probably built to keep animals away rather than human beings.

Robert appeared eager to get inside and was already looking for what looks an entrance. He found one by the right side, and he beckoned to Alice to come. They went through the wooden fence and they found the door to the chalet. Robert tried the doorknob but it would not budge. Alice looked through the window maybe she could find someone inside the chalet, but apart from logs of woods, a dining tableland a fireplace, she did not see anything.

“Let’s look around, maybe we can find the key. The key is usually kept around.” Alice suggested.

The first place they checked was the foot mat at the entrance. Plumes of dust rose in the air when Alice lifted it. However, there was no key underneath. She searched the clay bucket with the flower next but she did not see it there.

"Let's check the side. If we don't see the key, then we can watch out for an open window or something." Alice suggested further.

They went around the chalet looking for an open window or another entrance. Robert saw wood that was wide as a door by the side of the chalet. It was probably an old door. Robert lifted it and checked its shade maybe they would find the key into the chalet there. It was not there. They moved to the back and they found a window but it was closed.

Robert knew that if he carried Alice on his shoulder, her hands would reach it and she can try the window. If it opened, then they have an entrance. However, he did not want to suggest it. She had all of her trousers kissing flowers and dirt all day and he could not imagine allowing her to rub that on his Armani suit.

"Here is a window," Alice pointed.

"Yes, but it is high for any of us to reach it. Did you see a ladder or something?"

"No. I guess we go back to the door and knock or wait till the owner comes back."

"What if the owner doesn't come back? Isn't a chalet seasonally sort of? I might not know much about nature but I know this."

It was Alice turn to be quiet. She knew right from the time that the chalet would be empty by this time of the year. Most of the cattle herder who owned the chalet would have moved back to the low valleys before the onset of the alpine winter. Nevertheless, she had her reservations about breaking into another person's property.

She had come from a big family. She had three older siblings and two younger ones. They usually had loads of fun together. In the morning, they went to school and in the afternoon, they returned and went mountain hiking, playing several games on the way. They would be off home for several hours and their parents were sure they would be back before dinner.

One day, Alice returned from school feeling tired so she opted out of the ritual mountain hiking and decided to rest instead. That evening, his siblings returned without the youngest of them, Luca. They waited until time for dinner with hopes that he would be back. He did not come back.

Consequentially, a search party set out to look for him. They search the mountains and the valleys, but they did not find him. A section of the search party went to the nearest town to look for him. Police printed a missing person poster and the search for Luca was on.

It was not until the third day before they found him. They found him in a chalet at the edge of the town. His body had been dismembered. He had been blown to pieces. He had attempted to enter the chalet out of curiosity perhaps, but he would not know the owner had secured it with a tripwire because he had stored his dead wife's golden trinkets and earrings inside.

Luca's death put a hold on their freedom and caused a fear of breaking into an unknown property in her mind.

Therefore, when Robert suggested they break into the chalet, Luca's memories came flooding her mind and she remembered the grotesque view of the dismembered body parts of her late brother.

"I don't support you breaking in." Alice voiced her opinion.

"But you would support us dying out here in the cold?" Robert walked forward towards the door. "I am breaking down this door and don't try to stop me."

Alice could not stop him so she stepped back. She feared there would be tripwire at the doorway and it would explode like the one that killed Luca. She watched him as he went towards the door. He tried the knob once again, but it was still the same, so he went back and gathered pace then he slammed his body into the door.

The door creaked and part of it gave way. Robert went back once more and slammed his foot on the remaining parts of the door. It broke into pieces. He used his hands to remove the remaining parts that blocked the entrance. Then he stepped inside-Into Alice's fear.

Chapter Four

Alice's fear did not materialize. She went in after him.

The chalet was a single room that was the combination of a bedroom, a dining room, and a kitchen. A king sized bed was a the northwest of the room near the window, while an oval shaped dining table with a set of four chairs was on the opposite side. A fireplace, with a black netted gate, was in the middle of the chalet. A table with rafter basket that contained chopped logs of wood was parallel to the fireplace and it was directly opposite the entrance.

The inside of the chalet was dusty in contrast to the outside ambient which was cold. Several strings of cob-webs ran from the table to the fireplace, around the dining table, from the unopened windows and at the edges of the walls. Robert's countenance changed immediately he saw the dust and cobwebs. He stood glued to a spot. Alice stepped outside and took a piece of wood from the door Robert had broken down and used it to destroy the cob-webs.

"How can someone live in a house so dusty?"

'The owner can live in his house as he wills. Moreover, he didn't invite you inside. You broke in remember."

"It is 'we' that broke in. Emphasis on the 'We.' Remem-ber you are inside without authorization."

Alice found an old piece of cloth on a chair at the dining table. She picked it up, and a suggestion came to her mind.

"I would dust the room, but you go and look for something we can use to cover the door since you have broken the original one."

Robert would not have this. He wanted to search the chalet for a working phone, but from the look at the dust and all, he doubts if he could find a phone that worked. At the pretense of looking for something to stand in place of a door, he searched around the chalet for a phone. It was an old-fashioned interior, as everything looked out of date. The king-sized bed had springs instead of pure foam; the shape of the carving on the dining table was old and out of fashion; there were also buckets and pots which were made from iron as against aluminum that was now in use.

There was no phone in the chalet and Robert was disappointed, but he did not show it. He decided if he could pass the night here, maybe tomorrow, he would walk around and search the surroundings. He could find a chalet someone was staying in or someone with a phone.

Then it occurred to him. There was wood, by the side of the chalet, which he had lifted when they were looking for the key to open the door. The wood would fit into the door space and act as a door. He went to the side of the chalet, carried the door and brought it to the front of the chalet. He placed it near the door's threshold. Whenever they needed to close the door, he would lift the door and use it to block the door.

There was a new another problem he discovered. The chalet had no electricity. Although he could see wire connections and a bulb, the switch on the wall does not switch it on. He was not adept that those kinds of things. He never had to do anything in Zurich. Now he had to find a way to fix the electricity. He had seen the electrician come around whenever he had a small electrical problem in the office or at home.

Like that day he was working late in the midnight and the lights just went out. He needed to close a deal before midnight and it was thirty minutes to midnight. He stood up and looked out through the window to check if it was just his building or the general city. The other buildings had power so it was only his building. He did not have the time to check around the house, even if he had the time, he did not know what to do. Therefore, he switched on the torchlight application of his Smartphone to finish the work he was unto, and then look for a solution to the power when he was through.

As he set to work on his Mac book, a warning battery notification came on the screen. Less than 10% battery left!

A sudden fear shrouded his heart. Because of the seriousness of his work, he had forgotten to charge the laptop battery. He had to fix the power.

He picked up his phone and called his electrician. It would be later before he realized it was odd for him to call at that time. The electrician picked up the call but he was at the hospital and his wife was in labor. Robert would have to wait until morning before he could come.

Robert could not wait until morning, so he opened Google search engine and he searched for the keywords: Sudden power cut possible solutions. A thousand answers with bold clickable links showed up. He clicked the first one after reading the first few words. The link opened to an article that had a video attached. The article talked about a fuse box that acts as a guard, and it had a self-destructive mechanism to stop the flow of electricity if it detects an anomaly. It explained the components of a fuse box and what will happen when it tripped off. The video attached at the bottom of the article showed how to repair a fuse by reconnecting the positive and negative ends with a new wire.

After re-watching the video until the Mac book shut down by itself because of low power, Robert was convinced he could repair the fuse and restore power to the office again. He took his phone and used it as torchlight, and he went out of his office, down the stairs, down the corridor into the electrical room. He was able to identify the fuse as from the video he had just seen.

He touched the fuse, and he attempted to pull it out as shown in the video. He would never know what happened as he felt a surge that immobilized him and moving around his body in jet speed. He saw spirals and more spirals until everything became blank.

He spent two weeks in the hospital for a concussion and electrical shock. Since then, he never went near anything that breaths in electricity.

This was another scenario and he would not want the previous experience to happen again. Alice had finished dusting the room, but it past twilight outside.

"Could you connect the electrical cable?" Alice asked. She had noticed a wire from a small installation of solar panels nearby.

Robert felt been enveloped by fear. From the way Alice has said it, it appeared as if it is something casual, something she can fix, but she just wants him to have the share of the job. He walked outside the chatel without having the slightest idea of what to do. If their phones weren't dead, he would have searched for it on Google. Now that was not even a possibility because if he had a phone, he would have called for help and they would probably be in a helicopter by now.

"It is getting dark in here, I can't see anything." Alice's voice rang out from the chatel.

Robert would hate to admit to Alice that he does not know how to do what she was asking him. He does not want to lose his prestige in her sight. That is even if he had any prestige. After all, all he had done since their path crossed was to shine his headlights at her, then honk when she didn't respond till it provoked her to stop, then not thanking her because he was more focused on getting to Zurich, then crashing into her when they were coming to the chalet.

Alice wondered what sort of man Robert was. Her best guess was that he was an intolerant person and is the very ignorant person on basic things. She had finished cleaning out the dust and cobwebs from the chalet, and she needed light to see the other things in place. She was famished and she was hoping there was something in the chalet that they could cook and eat. Getting impatient, she went outside the chalet towards the electrical connection at the back of the chalet.

She met Robert by the side of the chalet, idling away as if he really had nothing to do.

"If we continue like this, we will get nowhere," Alice complained.

"I was—"

Alice stretched her opened palm towards his mouth before he could finish, then she swiveled and went in the direction of where the electric cable usually was. Having found the cable, it took her few seconds to find the socket at the back of the chalet. She connected it and light drowned the darkness that had swallowed the chalet.

She walked back angrily past Robert on her way into the chalet.

Robert felt he needed to clear the air. His silence might just be a recipe for disaster. Even though he was not used to someone talking down to him like Alice had been doing all evening, he knew he did not have a choice. This was not his world. It does not seem like he would get out of the area at least until the following day. He needed to survive the night. Holding his surrender, he walked into the chalet.

Alice seemed to be looking for something.

"What are you looking for?"

"I am famished." She answered without looking at his face.

She had made a valuable point. He was famished too, but the hope that he would get to Zurich that night had pushed the thoughts on what to eat out of his mind.

He joined her and they rummaged every single cupboard in the chalet. In the end, Alice found some rice inside a barrel near the fireplace while Robert saw a pre-cooked soup in sachets. Several pots were near the fireplace and they were lucky one of the several barrels near the dining table was filled with clean water. Alice gathered the things they had found and brought them near the fireplace.

The night was upon them and the cold had descended. It was blowing into the chalet through the door. Without being told, Robert went outside the chalet and lifted the piece of wood he had seen earlier and he used it to block the door.

Alice looked up from the things they had gathered. "We need a matchbox to make fire."

Robert smiled. "I bet with all my stakes that we would find a match in this chalet."

Robert was 100% sure there has to be a match somewhere. He once had a Bulgarian client, Mr. Miroslav, who invited him over to Sofia to finalize a business deal. Looking out of the window on the trip from Sofia airport to Mr. Miroslav apartment in Athens Street, he was surprised to find many people smoking out in the open. He let out his surprise when he reached Mr. Miroslav apartment.

"Don't you know that after Serbia, we are next in the list of the country that smokes most in the world?" He picked up a cigarette and he offered one to Robert. He declined. "In almost all homes in Sofia, there are two things you would always find: an ashtray and a lighter. In fact, any house you see with an ashtray, there got to be a lighter hidden somewhere." He took a lighter out of his pockets and he lit the cigarette.

Robert had seen an ashtray on the dining table when they were rummaging the chalet for food, so he was sure there had to be a lighter or match box somewhere. He started looking.

Alice was dumbfounded after she heard Robert saying he bet all his stakes on finding a matchbox. Someone that did not know how and where to connect the electrical cable would be the one to know where the matchbox is. The world never ceased to amaze one with the people in it.

Robert found it. It was underneath the bed. It must have fallen off from the small cupboard near the bed.

"Here is it." He stretched it forth to Alice.

Alice collected it. She was flabbergasted. She had never imagined Robert could be useful for anything, but finally, he did find himself useful where Alice was hopeless.

She placed some of the logs into the fireplace and she made fire with the aid of the matchbox. Then she washed some rice and put them to boil in a pot that she placed in the fireplace. Meanwhile, Robert sat down and looked back in retrospect at the day. He had never imagined this strings of incidents would happen. A thirty-five million dollars business deal was going down the drain and there was nothing he could do to stop it.

Maybe I should not have been so secretive about it.

He had played with his cards close to his chest in getting this deal. His staffs knew something was coming, but they did not know the client or the amount of money involved. Robert ensured that.

Of recent, he had been suspecting that his major competitor, the Weinsteins, had placed a mole within his company but he couldn't figure it out, even though he hired a private detective to run background checks on all his staffs. They all came clean. He still believed in his mole theory. He had the gut feeling someone has been too smart.

The deal was the biggest he would ever engage in and he feared that if he let out the details, the mole would tell his employers and they would steal they deal from him. He had eyes on Sharon, his secretary of five years. Lately, she had been paying special attention to the account section-something that did not concern her. He even caught her eavesdropping on a conversation he was having with a female client whom he was escorting to her car.

Now he felt if he had told his staffs, they would have filled in for him and picked up Mr Ocean from the airport. But now, it was too late.

The door fell all of a sudden and a gush of wind blew into the chalet, sending the chandelier over the dining table to a swinging mission and almost blowing out the fire in the fireplace.

"We would have frequent winds like that." Alice said, blowing the fire with a small plastic plate to rekindle it. "You need to put something heavy at the back of the door."

"But I can't put it from inside."

Alice stood up and pointed to the window. "You would open the window from inside, carry some of the barrels outside and use it to secure the door, and then place one near the window so that you can use it to climb in."

Alice was right, Robert thought. That was the only way the door could hold. With Alice's help, they both rolled six of the barrels near the dining table outside. The barrels were heavy and sealed, so they had to roll them.

Then he went outside. He put the door in place and then he placed three barrels on the floor to hold the door in place. Then another two barrels on top the three, then one barrel on top. The door should now be able to withstand the wind surges, he thought. He rolled the remaining barrel on to the back of the chalet and he placed it near the window. He was about to climb it when he saw something glowing in the dark. He was able. It was another form of life outside there-perhaps a man.

"Who is there?" His voice rang out and echoed back to him.

Then he heard a shuffle. Like a race within the field. This was no human. It could be an animal, a wild animal. He climbed on top the barrel in haste and attempted to enter through the window. The window was still high for him to enter without any fuss, but he was not having any of that with an unknown animal racing towards him from the field.

He had entered halfway. His torso was through the window while his legs were dangling outside the window.

"Help," He screamed.

Alice heard Robert's voice. She stood up from the fireplace and went to the window where the voice was coming from. She could not help but laughed when she saw Robert flailing her arms and crying for help.

She went to him, pulled him and helped him get inside, and then she continued laughing.

"But made you hang by the window when you know the barrel height wasn't enough to make you enter through the windows easily." She was still laughing.

Robert wanted to show anger, but there was this feeling of a veiled comedy around the incident.

"I hear something running towards me from the field. So I quickly jumped, fearing it might be a dangerous animal."

This caused Alice to laugh even more and Robert's initial bottled anger was now rising.

"I bet the wild animal you heard running towards you was an Ibex." Then she continued laughing as she walked back to the fireplace.

Robert did not say a thing. He stood and dusted the dirt that had clung to his suit, pants and shoes with his palms. Then he went to sit on the dining table.

Meanwhile, Alice had stopped laughing soon after she returned to the fireplace. The rice was ready, so she took the pot off the fire, while she made the pre-cooked soup in another pot and she warmed it. The food was soon ready and she served it on two plates.

Robert and Alice sat in opposite positions on the dining table and they ate slowly and shrouded in silence. Robert was still fuming that he failed to make it to Zurich in time to meet Mr Ocean, while Alice felt indifferent about not being able to go home, instead she felt unfortunate to be paired in here with a cocky, ungrateful clown who thought he was a gentleman.

"Could you pass the salt?" Robert requested, pointing to the salt shaker near Alice.

She passed the saltshaker to him. She watched as he sprinkled the salt into the soup.

"Do you always add extra salt to your food?"

"Yes," He answered with a deliberate slur in his voice, still sprinkling the salt as he answered.

"You know it could lead to hypertension over time."

"You don't look like a nurse."

"I don't have to be a nurse to know some basic health tips."

They continued the rest of the meal in silence. After the meal, Alice cleared the plates together and placed them in a heap on the dining table.

Robert watched her and wondered what could be going on through her mind. She did not look bothered about being trapped and not able to go home. She showed no fear about having to share a chalet with a strange man for the night and perhaps another night until they could figure out a way to call for help.

"You don't seem bothered. Are you an orphan?"

"Well, in Zurich, do you call someone with three older siblings and two younger ones an orphan?"

"A big family it is." Robert said. "And they won't be bothered about not seeing you?"

Alice was silent. For the first time since the avalanche, it hit her- her family would be hyper-worried. She did know that, but she was doing all she could do bottle it and enjoy the moment. Julian had texted her when she was driving about the time she would be home. She wondered what her family would look like. After probably calling her number endlessly without success, they might be nursing fear she had met a similar fate as her younger brother, Luca, who was blown after his legs pulled a tripwire guarding a chalet. They would probably have launched a search party to look for her.

"Helloooo?"

She could see hands waving across her eyes and it drew her from her thoughts. "They would be worried, but I'm helpless. I once read that worrying is like a rocking chair. It gives you work to do but takes you nowhere."

"I don't agree." Robert sat his jaws on his opened palms with elbows resting on the dining table. "Sometimes, worrying could pave the way for a solution."

"Like yours has paved one for you?"

"You don't understand. I can't be on the verge of losing a business deal of thirty million dollars without giving it serious thought."

"Thirty million dollars! That is quite a lot of money. How come you are losing it?"

Robert explained everything to her. From his suspicion of a mole in his office to the manner in which he played the cards of the latest business deal close to his chest.

Alice breathed out. "Have you ever heard of hope?"

"Hope as in the deal might still be on?"

"Hope is a good thing; maybe the best of things and no good thing ever dies."

"That sounds like a quote."

"Yes, it is from my favorite movie- The Shawshank Redemption. Have you seen it?"

Robert shook his head.

"Wait, do you watch movies at all?"

Robert shook his head again. "This favorite film of yours, The Shaw-"

"-Shank Redemption."

"Thanks. How does it relate to my business deal?"

"Since you haven't seen the movie, let me give you a concise version of the film"

Robert adjusted his posture a bit and set his gaze on Alice's face.

'Well, a man called Andy Dufresne was sentenced to Shawshank for killing his wife. He made friend with Red who smuggles things and sell them in prison. Both of them became good friends. He asked Red to help him get a small rock hammer for carving miniature statues and a Rita Hayworth wall poster. Red got them for him and life moved on.

Years later, Tommy Williams became an inmate. Andy became friends with Tommy and he tutored him to pass his GED exams.

One day, Tommy Williams mentioned that he was once inmate with a convict who confessed to killing a man and his drunken banker husband took the rap for it. Andy realized it was his own case, so he told the warden about it. The warden did not want him to leave because Andy was doing shady deals for the warden at that time.

The following morning, someone found William dead. The warden said he was trying to escape so he was shot dead. The inmates knew the warden was lying, but no one talked.

Many years later, during a routine cell check, Andy's cell was empty."

Robert stretched his hand to make her pause. "Let me guess, he escaped?"

"That's right. He had been digging a tunnel right underneath the Rita Hayworth's poster. And he escaped through it."

"It has a very good plot. I should see it when I get back to Zurich."

"I am surprised. You don't watch movies. So what do you do apart from work?"

"I read books."

"Novels?"

"Yes, I read them too."

"You have a favorite?"

"The Godfather by Mario Puzo."

"Damn."

"You have not read it?"

"You bet not. I have read it over five times. Mario Puzo took and examined the life of Don Corleone from twelve years old till he died, then he moved to his son, Michael."

"You are a voracious reader then." Robert stood. "I saw a novel when I wanted to pick the matchbox, let me go and see." He went to the cupboard beside the bed and returned with a novel. "The Kite Runner by Khalid Hosseni." He said, stretching the novel towards Alice

She collected it from him. "Ooorrrhhh."

"Have you read it?"

"No, but I hear it is a very interesting novel about Taliban, family and life in general."

"I have read it, but it was a long time ago. I can barely remember the plot."

"If you had remembered, I would have asked you to narrate it like I had narrated The Shawshank Redemption. But –"

"What if I read it to you?" Robert suggested

Alice returned the novel to him. "Reading to me is such a nice idea." She stood. "Wait, let me clear the dishes. When I return, then you would start."

She stood and carried the dishes they had used to the table parallel to the fireplace. She had the aim of cleaning the dish the following morning, so she returned to the dining table to meet Robert who had already opened The Kite Runner to the first chapter.

He started reading, "I became what I am today at the age of twelve, on a frigid overcast day in the winter of 1975…"

At first, Alice was attentive to Robert's crisp voice, and then worry took her on a voyage back to Kandersteg. She drew a mental picture of what her house might be looking like at that moment. She was sure the search parties would have returned from the search with plans to continue the following day. Her hypertensive father would surely have his blood literally boiling and it would be a stroke of luck if his blood pressure weren't already at an abnormal level. Her mother would probably refuse to use her diabetic drugs and she would spend all night brooding. Her siblings would be confused about the whole scenario because she was a role model to them and they would not be able to fathom what is happening to her. Julian would try his best to tell them he had texted her that evening but she did not reply. She was probably driving and that was why she did not reply. She was probably struck on the road and it was getting dark, so she decided to stay in a Hotel. Her mother would not accept it and she would pelt Julian with questions about the holes in his narration. They would ask her which Hotel does not have a telephone. She would ask him how long it took to drive from that particular place in Swiss Alps to Kandersteg. She would mention Leon, their next-door neighbor who just arrived from Zurich, which was farther than that place.

Alice felt a hand tapping her. "You are sleeping already."

Somnolence still held reign over her eyes. "I sorry I drifted off. I am tired."

"Me too. It had been a long day."

Alice stood and Robert stood after her. She walked away from the dining table, past the fireplace to the bed. Then she realized the one problem that had been with them all along. There was only a single bed in the room.

She could not think of what they could do, so she fell on the bed, making sure there was enough space for Robert.

Robert came along and he fell on the space Alice had left for him. He did not bother to take off his suit or shoes. Soon, he was snoring.

Chapter Five

The next morning, Alice was the first to wake up. Robert was still sleeping. She was surprised to see him still dressed in his suit, and more surprised to see him wearing his shoes.

She went to the door and wanted to go out when she remembered the improvisation Robert had done with the door. She could not leave unless they opened it from outside. She would have loved to open it, but she could not climb the window, so she opted to wait until when Robert woke up. She decided to cook them something instead.

She went to the barrel when she had found rice the previous night to get some rice, then she discovered the next problem they would face if they didn't find a way to call for help.

Hunger!

The rice remaining would barely be enough for them that morning. They had better find help or food when Robert woke up. She got to work and cooked the remaining rice.

Robert woke up when she was making the pre-cooked soup. The first thing he noticed when his feet kissed the ground was the cold that entered through his heels.

His shoes!

His first thought was that Alice had stolen them and ran away. He used his hands to feel this pocket for wallet maybe she took them too. A sound of metal clanging from the fireplace drowned his fears. Alice was still much around.

It must be a thief then.

He stood and went to find Alice.

"We need to get away from this place."

"What do you mean?"

"Look at my legs."

Alice set her gaze on his legs. She felt he looked funnier without his shoes on, so she burst out laughing.

"You think this is funny?"

Alice was still laughing while Robert was getting furious.

"I was the one who took your shoes."

"You think this is some sort of joke?"

Alice could see his face toughened with angry and his hands balled.

She stopped laughing, "I took it off when I woke up and discovered you had slept with them." She pointed towards the bed. "I kept them under the bed."

Robert went to bed and checked underneath it. He retrieved his shoe, wore then and walked back to Alice.

"Toothbrush and paste."

"Are you asking me? You forget too soon we are like a terrorist in someone else's house."

"This isn't fit to be called a home."

"Whatever. We have serious problems on our hands. First, I need you to open the door."

Robert rolled a barrel towards the window, climbed on it and went out through the window. Then he went to the entrance, dismantled the barrels he had used to secure the door and he opened it.

Alice was waiting by the door with plates in her hands by the time Robert opened the door. She took them out, and then she took some water and used it to rinse the plates because she could not find a sponge and soap.

When she returned to the room, Robert was sitting on a chair by the dining table.

"Take some water to rinse your mouth. Use a finger to clean your teeth and tongue while at it. That's the best we can do out here."

Robert felt bad. No brush and toothpaste or mouth rinse. He could not remember the last time he ate breakfast without brushing his teeth, not to forget the quarterly visits to the dentist. However, out here, the option Alice had offered him sounded well. He stood and went to rinse his mouth outside.

Alice served the rice she had cooked on the plates she just rinsed and she took it to the dining table. Then she took some water outside to rinse her mouth as if she had advised Robert to do.

After few minutes, both of them were back at the dining table.

"An idea came to me while I was brushing."

"No, not now. We talk when we finish eating."

Therefore, they ate in silence.

When they were through, Robert helped Alice carry the dishes outside where she rinsed them as she had done earlier in the morning. They then returned to the dining table.

"Now, let us talk about the problems. You wanted to say something earlier on."

'Yes," Robert said, he breathed out and continued. "We need to look for help so we can get back to our respective homes."

"Okay. And how do you suggest we do that?"

"We go back to the small mountain road. We may be lucky to see a car and we can hike it back to where we were coming from. We could make a distress call and or I could call Barkley and he would send a helicopter to us."

"So what if we don't see a car? Then all the plans would fall like a pack of cards. We would be back here and hunger would almost finish us."

"What?"

'The rice is finished. Even the water supply is running low."

"That's the more reason why we have to go to the road and seek help." Robert could see that Alice's face showed no excitement. "Or you don't agree with me?"

"I think we should look for food instead. Cars do not frequently show up here. It was just pure coincidence that both of us were on the same road at the same time."

"So what do you suggest?"

"I think we should look for food instead. Around the chalets, there is usually a *mazot* where the owners store food and water that they use during winter months."

Robert thought of it. She was right. He could not remember seeing any other car apart from that of Alice when he was driving. Still, he could not give up his search for help. Robert thought for a while.

"Remember you told me, hope is a good thing, maybe the best of all things, and no good thing ever dies."

Alice smiled. "Okay, I will follow you to the road, but we can't be there all day. We would stay there until midday and leave there if we do not see any help, then we channel all efforts into looking for a *mazot* and maybe a way to charge my phone.

Robert felt it seemed like a nice plan, but he hoped they would never have to come back to the chalet. She had mentioned until midday, and he was sure they would see a car before the time lapsed.

They ensured everything else was in place. Alice wanted her or him to write a note on the table should in case the owner of the chalet come back and met his door broken, but there was no pen or paper in sight.

Lastly, they disconnected the electricity cable and they replaced the door and held it in place with the barrels like Robert had done the night before. Then they started walking through the field to the road.

Alice could not believe herself. She had spent the night with a total stranger. Apart from his name and that he was going to Zurich; she knew nothing else about him.

"It is funny you know, apart from your name, I know nothing about you." Alice expressed her fears.

"It is the same here too. I only know you are Alice and from Kandersteg and also that you are a great cook."

Alice blushed.

"Well, as you know. I am Robert Jules. I live in Zurich. I am a finance expert and I am forty years old."

"Forty!"

"Do I look younger?"

"No, I thought you were in your early fifties."

Robert laughed. "I would be so in eleven years to come."

Alice plugged a flower and perceived its fragrance. She put her hands forward towards Robert's nose. "I don't know why you don't like flowers."

"I used to like them but I stopped?"

"Why?"

"It is a long story."

"Well, we have a long journey ahead of us. You might as well use it to fill in the gaps."

Alice was asking him to open the doors to the memories he had shut for nearly twelve years. He had never told anyone the story.

'It all started with my wife."

Alice was surprised. "You are married? I searched your finger for a ring yesterday but I didn't see one."

"I used to be married."

'Did she leave?"

"You have to be patient. You asked me to tell you."

Alice drew her hand across her mouth in gesturing that her mouth was now zipped close.

"Lucia is her name." Robert opened his wallet and brought out a passport photograph he had tucked in a compartment. "He gave it to Alice."

"She is beautiful." Alice returned it to him

"That's my wife. We got married when I was twenty-five years old. We had been lovers since high school. We both gained admission into the University of Basel and our love waxed stronger as the year wafted past. Six years later, we were married in a colorful wedding ceremony.

Lucia came from a rich banking family that controlled three of the biggest financial institutions in Geneva. After my marriage to her, I was quickly promoted to be the manager of one of the banks the family controlled.

Our marriage was the best thing that ever happened to us. We did most things together. Lucia would not eat until I returned from work; I would not sleep until she was through with her television programs; we would not bathe unless in the company of one another. The only thing that separated us was work and her family made sure I got the minimum time required for the job."

"So what happened? This story looks perfect so far." Alice said.

"It was perfect," Robert paused a bit, "very perfect. I came back from work one evening and Lucia broke the surprising news to me. It was the best thing I had heard in my life. She was pregnant. My joy was boundless and I screamed so loud that people heard it several blocks away. To show how loud my scream was, the police visited shortly afterward and told us there was a report of a disturbance from my property. I told them I was joyous and I would not disturb the neighbors again.

The news heightened my love for her. I forbade her from entering the kitchen or doing any strenuous once she finished her first trimester. We had a house cleaner who came around every day though, but Lucia insisted she wanted to be the one to cook my meals. I tried my best to stop her. I would instruct the house cleaner not to allow my wife stress herself, but once I went to work, my wife was the boss and the house cleaner had no choice but to obey her instructions.

Every Friday, I brought flowers for Lucia. She loved them and was usually appreciative. It started as an honest show of love, and then it turned ritual.

On a Friday, I was already near our home when I discovered I had forgotten to buy flowers. The work that day overwhelmed me that I was tired and that made me forgot. Without entering the house, I reversed and went to buy flowers. When I returned, I realized it was the greatest mistake I would ever make in my life."

Roberts's eyes were moist and tears began to flow without control. Alice used her hand to clean the tears from his cheeks.

"Maybe you should stop."

"No, I already started," he used his palms to wipe the remaining tears dry, "I will finish it."

'If only I knew, I wouldn't have gone to buy the flowers. I would have prevented the disaster from happening.

The house was on fire when I returned."

"Wow." It was Alice's turn to show display of feelings. She was astonished. She could never imagine Robert having a life so beautiful and envious.

"The fire department was quick to come but it was too late for my wife and unborn child. The smokes suffocated them to death.

I cried as I had never done before. The fire had destroyed all the happiness I had in life. If only I did not turn back.

My life took a pause after that. I spent so much time indoor deep in thoughts. After the burial, I thought to myself. No matter how much you worry, it would not bring your wife and kid back. So I decided to resume my life. That was when a salvo blow hit me. My father-in-law would not believe his daughter died by accident. He accused me of killing my wife to inherit her properties. I cried so hard, how would I kill someone I loved dearly?

Within the twinkle of an eye, I was sacked as the bank manager, all the properties that had affiliations with my wife's family were seized from me. I was left penniless."

Alice had tried since the beginning of the narration to bottle her questions but she could not hold them anymore.

"Why didn't the police get involved to exonerate you from the accusation your father-in-law aimed at you."

"The police never accused me of murder. Only my father-in-law did."

"But he had no right to collect all the properties."

"I was initially going to fight it out in court, but when I received death threats, I stopped. Then I told myself I would be rich."

"And you are." Alice tapped him on the shoulder. "You are a very strong man."

Robert felt like his heart had been relieved of a heavy load. He had never felt better in twelve years. He used his thumb and index finger to stroke his non-existent mustache. "I guess it is your turn to narrate. And I really hope you don't tell a story that would make me cry."

Alice smiled. "I'm Alice, thirty-five years old and I own a flour shop in Kandersteg."

"Married?"

Alice raised her left fingers to Robert's face. "The fourth finger has never worn a ring."

Robert had his reservations that she was not married. He had thought she was a divorcee, probably with a kid or two. Now he feared he would hear a story that would make him pity her more than himself.

"There is no story if you are expecting one."

"Not even one?"

"Not one. I have a great family and I reserve all my love for them."

"I have never known family for the past twelve years."

They were through with the flower field and were now on the path that knee-length shrubs and tall trees bordered.

"What happened to your own family? I thought it was your father-in-law who alienated you."

'That's true. I was the one who severed the ties with my family."

Alice's mouth was wide open and her palm was covering the opening. She was filled with surprise. This Robert story sure has turns and twists.

"When I announced to my family that I was marrying Lucia, they refused."

"Why?"

'Well, my elder brother had carried out a personal research and he told my parents that my father-in-law was a control freak and that he had maltreated one of his sons-in-law when his wife had a miscarriage.

I dismissed the idea then because Sonny was the son-in-law they were talking about. Sonny was a person whom the word bastard could only describe best and he was always cheating on his wife. There was even a time she called Lucia and asked her to intervene. Lucia and I went to her house but Sonny would not allow us into the house. He said it was not any of our business.

Therefore, I believe he deserved every treatment he received. I was confident something like that would not befall me because I sincerely loved Lucia and I explained it to my family, but they were adamant. I was adamant too that I would marry Lucia with or without their support.

My families were of the opinion that the reason why I was adamant was that Lucia's family was rich and that was what attracted me. There was no way I was going to make them see the other way.

I married Lucia without any of their support. Only my youngest brother, Levin, attended my wedding. Also, he was with us for a while, always checking us every now and then until he just stopped coming. I guess the family pressure on him was high."

"What of your brother, the one who did the research.. em."

"Elias."

"Yes, Elias. I felt he should have understood you more, and even after your family-in-law ousted you, he should have taken you in."

"Well, Elias didn't do anything. They all told me that they warned me. It was a case of he who laughs last laugh best."

They were now on the road. It was the same way they had left it: the bare asphalted single lane road with the Alps bordering it on the side and the cold mountain air that descended giving it a distinct smell. They walked to where the accident had happened and as Alice predicted, it was still the same way. There was no sign anyone had come there.

"Didn't I tell you?"

"You did, and you made a promise we would stay until midday then we pursue what you have in mind."

"Okay, fair enough."

The sun was coming out and soon its ray would be unbecoming for their skins, so Alice suggested they walked to the side where trees were, get something to sit and watch out for any help.

They found a log near the path they had just walked passed through and they rolled it to the edge of the road. They positioned it at the edge of the road where the tall trees provided shade, before the bend, so that they would have a good view of any incoming vehicle for quite a good distance.

They had barely sat down when Alice began her questions.

"Your brother, Elias, where is he now?"

"He is somewhere in Gruyeres. I heard he works in a chocolate factory there."

Robert felt he was talking too much about himself. Alice had not really said much about herself and he had the feeling she also had a lot bottled up.

'What about your own brother?"

"You mean Luca?"

"Yes Luca."

"Sorry, I mean to say Julian."

Robert could hear her change in tone. Alice was trying to hide something. One cannot forget the name of his brother.

"No, I mean Luca. Remember I told you a story I had not told anyone for twelve years."

It was true. Alice had not told anyone Luca's story. There was no one he could tell though. She had lived all her life in Kandersteg and all the inhabitants of the town knew the story.

'Luca is my brother, but he is dead."

"Wow, I am sorry."

"You don't have to be. I am sorry I don't have a photo to show you like you did with Lucia. Remember yesterday when you wanted to break the door to the chalet and I objected to it?

"Yes, it infuriated me."

"You have every right to and I had every reason to stop you. That was how Luca died."

Alice went on and told Robert in details how Luca had found a chalet and he broke into it only for him to trip a wire and he was blown to pieces.

Robert felt a ripple of shock running through his body at lightning speed. He could have been blown to pieces!

Alice could see the red on Robert's face.

"In truth, most chalets don't have that kind of dangerous security. The one Luca tripped happened to be one in which the owner had some valuables in them and he wanted to secure them."

Robert felt ease, but he still thought there could have been a small probability that the chalet had a tripwire. He-something broke his thought. He heard something. The sound was distinct. So distinct that it could get them out of there.

A helicopter

He jumped from the log he was sitting on and ran in the direction of the sound while pulling off his suit.

Robert was off and running before Alice could hear it. She rose and went after Robert.

Robert was screaming and swinging his suit and running at the same time. The helicopter was far off in the sky, but Robert never ran out of hope. All he needed was the pilot of the helicopter to see the waving of his suit. He could rudder the helicopter and come to their rescue.

Alice had removed her jacket and she was swinging it alongside the screams they were now both making. They kept on swinging and screaming until the sound and sight of the helicopter disappeared into the mountain clouds.

"And this was our chance." Robert used his suit to hit the asphalted covered road in anger.

"Maybe fate has other things in stock for us." Alice checked the time. "It is ten minutes to midday. Do you want to wait or should we go and look for a *mazot*."

'Let's run the ten minutes out. Who knows, the pilot may have seen something."

"Yes, no good thing ever dies."

"Yes, you taught me that."

They waited the ten minutes in a silence that was filled with anxiety. There was no helicopter propeller sound, only the occasional zephyrs from the mountain ranges whistling in the afternoon sun.

"Ten minutes is over." Alice said, pointing to her wristwatch. "I could be generous and add ten more minutes."

Robert smiled. "We better get going."

They walked back through the path they had walked through earlier in the morning, unto the field and then into the chalet.

"I can really use the ten minutes now," Robert said, setting down the barrel they had used to secure the door close. "Let's rest for ten minutes, gather our thoughts and plan, and then go search for the *mazot*."

"Okay."

They entered the hut and sat on the dining table. Alice took some water in cups for both of them.

"Is this how we would always be trapped here?" Robert said after he drank a mouthful of water.

"No, it would only take a few days. Help would come."

"Only if we had a phone."

"We have to remember, the power is dead."

"That is true, and we have electricity too. We could look for a way to charge it."

"Look who's talking. One who is scared of electricity. We have a better chance of an ibex walking through the eye of a needle than you finding a way we could charge this phone without a charger."

Robert was silent. Alice had spoken the truth. Ever since the incident at his office, he hated anything that dealt with electricity. But now, he had to bury his fears if he was to have a good chance at getting out of there.

Alice stood. "I think we have had enough rest. Let's go look for a *mazot*."

Robert stood from the chair and they both went outside the chalet. They secured it close to the wood and barrels like they had been doing and they set off.

"Which direction do we go?" Robert asked

"The *mazot* should be around. Let us go towards the direction the back of the chalet pointed."

The direction Alice had chosen was the most logical one, Robert thought. The left side of the chalet opened to the flower field where the path that led to the highway was. The right-hand side was about five hundred meters from a valley. A small piece of land and the valley bordered the front side. The only logical direction was the back of the chalet.

They went to the back with Alice somewhat leading the way. There was a problem though, there was no path at the back like the type that led to the road.

Alice could see gloom on Robert's face.

She smiled. “I am sure there is a path somewhere here. The flowers must have covered it.” She went to the side of the chalet looking for a stick. She found a long one around her height lying down near the wooden fence that surrounded the chalet. She broke it into two and stretched one to Robert.

‘I suggest you follow my lead.”

Robert collected the stick. He did not know or have an idea of what they were going to do. He felt optimistic about the whole thing.

Alice led the way and she started using the stick she wielded to create a path in the field. Robert never thought of that. The idea was brilliant.

“How old are you?” Robert asked amidst the noise the stick was making as they created a path through the flower field.

“Thirty-five.”

“What!” Robert exclaimed and shock glued him to a spot. “You look twenty-five.”

Alice smiled. This was not the first time she would receive that compliment.

“Age is just a number.” She responded. She had stopped clearing the path for the small conversation.

"Age isn't just a number." He hit the flowers with the stick in a play motion. 'Your action, your mental reasoning and everything pointed to someone older. I just couldn't match it with your face."

'Thank you." She said and she continued clearing the path.

Alice had been noticing it since but she had dismissed it. Now she was very sure.

She stopped beating at the flower fields. She pointed to the ground. "Look, we are on a path. The flower was just covering it."

Robert could see it. There was indeed a path, but it was so obscure that one had to look carefully before noticing it.

"I am sure the *mazot* is nearby." Alice said with so much excitement shrouding her voice.

She was now hitting the flowers with so much vigor and power. Robert on the other hand had other thoughts in mind. The idea of losing the business deal with Mr Ocean had cooled in his mind. There was nothing he could do been trapped here, but he still hoped he could get to Zurich soonest. He was happy they were on a path that would definitely take them somewhere. A *mazot* like Alice had suspected? He does not know what it looked like but he hoped it could be modern sort of. Maybe they could see a phone that was working. Alternatively, they could see an abandoned phone charger.

He looked at Alice as she was clearing the path and he smiled. She had grown from a crazy woman to someone he was able to pour his mind to. No woman except Lucia had been able to pull that magic. Not even the great financial magnate, Ms Taylor. All the women he had come across after Lucia's death were both his work subordinates, and they shivered in his presence, and business partners whom he held a strong countenance to work with them.

"What are you thinking?"

Alice question caught him unaware and it sealed the gates of his thought.

"I hope we see a *mazot* that has a working phone."

Alice smiled. "It is true I told you the good thing about hope, but this one here is hopeless. *Mazots* are not designed for such."

'You mean."

"When we find it, you would understand."

It did not take them more than five minutes before they found the *mazot*. It was a small circular wooden hut with no windows. Its door was locked and Alice looked at Robert and she smiled.

"You are the specialist here." She stretched forth her opened palm and pointed to the *mazot* wooden door. "We have a door that needs to be hacked down."

Robert felt like he was wearing a suit of fear. The story of how Alice's brother was blown to pieces did send a chill down his spine. He had hoped he would have to break into a door ever in his life after hearing the Luca sad story.

"What if there is a tripwire behind the door."

Alice smiled. She did not think Robert would put his attention to her narration. She felt he must have been thinking about Zurich, his business dealings and how to get out of there the whole time. However, here is a testimony that he did listen.

"Trust me, there won't be any. Luca's case was just unfortunate and I bet you would never find another chalet with a tripwire guarding its doors in the whole Switzerland."

Robert did not move from his position.

"Okay, let us break it together, or better still, I will break it myself."

Robert would not have that. How would she be breaking the door while he stood there doing nothing.

"Don't worry, I got this."

"Are you sure?"

"Yes."

Robert stepped back and ran towards the door, crashing his shoulder unto the door. It bulged a bit. At the second try, the door fell off its hinges and fell inwards, taking Robert alongside it.

Alice ran to help him.

"Are you hurt?"

His shoulder hurt, but he would not show it. "No, I am fine." He got up.

The *mazot* was as Alice had said. Different kinds of food were stocked in it. There was rice in barrels, some wheat in bundles, several tins of evaporated milk, four sealed containers containing water, several sachets of pre-cooked soups and spaghetti in another barrel.

They decided to take what would be sufficient for them for the day, so they gathered some rice, a pack of spaghetti, and three sachets of pre-cooked soup and put them in an empty barrel. Alice carried that, while Robert carried one of the four water containers.

The trip back to the chalet felt shorter for both of them and they were silent for the better part of it. When they got back to the chalet, Alice got down to preparing something for them to eat while Robert sat on the dining table and he read 'The Kite Runner.'

Soon, lunch was ready and they ate. After they had finished eating and washed the plates, an idea came to Alice.

'Didn't the soup taste bland to you?"

Robert stroked his brows. "It did, but I bet I can't complain. We are in the middle of nowhere."

"I know you are not used to this. But we would soon get out of here."

'How soon do you think before rescue will arrive?"

"A week I guess."

"A week!" Robert exclaimed

"Aren't you glad we found a *mazot* with more than enough food to last us? If we had been struck without no food and shelter, then your exclamation would be appropriate."

Robert nodded. "It's true."

"What if we go and gather some mushroom later in the day to add to this soup. I saw many of them growing on the path to the small mountain road. I bet the taste would be sumptuous. And we get to eat it with spaghetti."

"Well, anything you cook is gold. So I believe you."

Silence reigned between them afterward. Robert struck to the novel while Alice removed her jacket, laid on the bed, and her thoughts won her over.

She imagined what would be happening at home. Her parents would have gone to report to the Police. Her mother would still refuse to eat until her daughter returned home. Her siblings would have an embargo placed on playing outside after school. Their house would host numerous visitors who would come to console the family as if she had died.

She now wondered what home would be like when she finally returned. She did not know if Robert would follow her home. They had been growing some kind of chemistry since they returned from the 'help hunt' they did on the road. If he did follow her home, her mother would be the happiest and her imaginations would run wild. She would conclude Alice had brought a husband. She paused and allowed her thought take a detour. Could she really marry Robert? She had been privy to see his heart and it was in huge contrast to the rude man she initially thought. He seemed like a good man, particularly from his narration of what happened between him and Lucia.

She wished she could get to share that kind of love with someone, but with whom? Robert? It was not a bad idea.

Robert was reading The Kite Runner. It had been a fantastic read and he followed the protagonist, Amir, through the streets of Kabul with his closest friend, Hassan, who was also the son of their servant. Amir would do the kite fight while Hassan, the kite runner, would do his best to outrun the other kite runners. Hassan had a good eye and a calculating brain, and he always knew where the kite would drop.

It had been a good read but Robert's mind soon drifted off back to Zurich. By the laws of nature, the business deal with Mr. Ocean should be off. However, there was something about what Alice had said on hope. He felt there had never been anything more truly.

There was something about Alice he had not yet understood. She was the reason why he was still alive. He imagined if he was the only one on the road when the avalanche happened. He would not have recognized the warning sound and boulders would have crushed him. His soul will be waiting for judgment if heaven and hell do exist.

Even if he somehow heard the warning sound, abandoned his car in haste and get into safety without a scratch, how would he survive. He did not have the idea a chalet would be around. Nonetheless, if he found the chalet on his own, the food was another thing. He had not cooked a meal for over fifteen years, not that he was even a good cook back then. Even if he knew how to cook, the food supply would have run out, he would have no idea something called a mazot is usually around a chalet, and that it is for food storage.

Robert took his gaze away from the pages of The Kite Runner and set them on Alice as she lay on the bed. She had been like an angel to him. The closest to Lucia he had ever seen. She had done more than he had done for her, and he started thinking maybe he should find a well-paying job for her when he returned to Zurich even if it means working with him in his office.

Before long, sleep carried them off. Alice lay gracefully on the bed while Robert placed his head on the pages of The Kite Runner and they both rest on the dining table

Chapter Six

Alice woke up. It was a nice sleep and her muscles felt relaxed. She stretched her hands and yawned. Her eyes went to the table when she had last seen Robert before she fell asleep. He was not there.

Maybe he is outside thinking about how to get to Zurich.

She got off the bed and went outside the chalet. Robert was not in sight. She looked around the chalet, but she could not find him. She returned inside.

Where could he have gone?

Several thoughts ran wild in her head. Had Robert seen a car or helicopter and decided to ditch her instead of alerting her? She quickly ditched the idea. There was no way how a helicopter would land without alerting her, even if it landed on the small road because she was a light sleeper and the slightest noise would wake her up?

Has he decided to go back to the road with hopes that he might see a car or a helicopter?

She grabbed her jacket without wearing it and she ran out the chalet. The path in the flower field was soon kissing her legs as she ran through. She had not run like this for a very long time save her she pulled Robert's hand and saved him from the avalanche. The last time she ran this fast was when the news filtered in from the search party to the town that they had found Luca's body. She sprinted so much that she could beat an Olympic medalist. Now she was racing for Robert!

She found him at the edge of the path with several mushrooms in his grip. She applied brakes to her sprinting feet and then she rested her hands on her knees and breathed out.

"Thank Goodness you are alright," Alice said, going forward to hug him.

"I was okay. I just thought I should help you gather the mushrooms you talked about." He opened his arms and accepted her hug.

"But you should have told me before you left. I was worried when I woke up."

"I am sorry," they were still locked in an embrace; "I didn't want to wake you up."

Alice had never felt such warmth for a long time. Her rhythm of her heartbeat returned to a normal cadence. A strange yet fulfilling ecstasy coursed through her body. She felt she was beginning to like Robert. Unbelievable.

Robert was not expecting a hug when Alice opened her arms towards him. When her luscious breasts pressed against his chest, the strange yet satisfying warmth that traveled through his body and it finally lodged in his abdomen region, tying playful knots with his intestines.

Alice broke from the embrace. "Let me see the mushroom you handpicked."

Robert opened his palms and he allowed Alice pick one of the mushrooms he had plucked from the moist ground and logs of wood.

Alice shook her head. "If we eat this, we would be dead by morning."

"What!"

Alice pulled Robert's hand, "Let me show you how to identify a poisonous mushroom."

She pulled him until they walked past the flower field and soon, they got to the path in the forest.

The mushrooms were on the rotten logs of wood by the edge of the path. She bent and plucked one, "Look here, this is how to recognize a mushroom that is poisonous. Avoid the ones with while gills," she pointed to the white gills, "you see them?"

"Yes. Poor me."

"That's not the only thing. You should also avoid mushrooms with red on its cap or stem, like this one." She bent and pointed to one that had red on its cap.

"Wow, I never knew mushrooms can be poisonous."

Alice had bent down and she was picking mushrooms that they would add to the soup. "Poisonous mushrooms can be very dangerous. There is even one called 'the death angel'

"Wow, like the angel of death. You don't need to explain it further, I understand."

Alice gathered the mushroom until they were a handful.

"I think these should be enough."

Then they turned and started walking back to the chalet.

"Tell me more about your brother."

"Elias?"

"Yes. I don't know but something seems to pique my interest in him."

"You want to marry him?" Robert said with a sarcastic laugh.

"Someone I have never met. It is not possible."

"It is. My secretary married her long heartthrob last year. And guess what, they met on Facebook. Then they exchanged contacts and they talked till love replaced the air they breathe."

Alice knew what Robert was doing, so she decided to beat him at his own game. "Well, that was on social media. What if I were to get Elias contact for instance, who knows what might blossom from there."

"Well he is married."

"Then we travel to a place where polygamy is allowed. Africa for instance or the Middle East. I have always wanted to live in Dubai."

'And who told you Elias can afford that."

"Why won't he. His brother is a financial mogul and he drives a Bentley."

Robert smiled. "What if I was lying? What if the Bentley was a rental car, and this handmade Armani suit and fancy shoes were just to impress a woman."

"Well, I'm a secret agent remember. You gave me that job."

Robert laughed and the sound drowned Alice's voice.

"Then I would know because I'm a sleuth." Alice continued.

"Like Miss Marple Jane?"

'Who is that?"

"Ever heard of Agatha Christie?"

"No. Never."

Robert's face was warped up by surprise "You don't know the mother of mystery?"

"I can't know all the novelists in the world."

"That is true, but there are some popular ones you have to know."

"Like Agatha Christie?"

"You know what, yesterday; you narrated The Shawshank Redemption for me. Today, I will narrate of Agatha Christie's best novel. I bet after you hear it, you would go and rummage bookstores in Kandersteg for her novels."

They were soon back at the chalet. The sun was almost entering its resting place and the curtain of darkness was slowly drawing over the skies. Alice went inside while Robert went to the back of the chalet to connect the electrical cable. He had hoped that for once he would defeat his electricity phobia.

He got to the back and he found the wire. He held it and moved it towards the socket, but when he got to the point of connecting it, all his bravery disappeared. Images of the electric shock he received at the office that night filled his thoughts.

The chalet was dark and Alice was having a tough time find the utensils she needed to cook.

What could be delaying Robert?

Alice dropped what she was doing and went out of the chalet to its backyard. She met Robert holding the electric cable. She did not say a thing to him. She just snatched the cable from his grip and she connected it. The light came on.

The light seemed to put life into Robert and his head went into a sudden jerk. "I am sorry, I should have—"

"Save it."

Alice was already walking back inside and Robert was following her at the back. She turned and suggested to Robert that he should put the barrels behind the door and come in through the window as he had done the previous night.

Robert was more than willing to pay for his gaffe. As soon as Alice entered, he replaced the door, secured it with barrels and he entered through the window. He did not hang there as he had done the previous nights, so there was no laughing from Alice who was busy cooking dinner.

He then went to sit on a chair by the dining table and he continued reading 'The Kite Runner.'

Dinner was soon ready and Alice served it. Spaghetti with soup with a moderate amount of mushroom added. They started eating.

"This mushroom is a revelation," Robert said excitedly, putting a fork full of spaghetti in his mouth.

'Yes, the mushroom made all the difference."

They ate the rest of the meal in silence.

When they were through, Robert insisted he packed the plates and he promised to wash them the following morning.

"I am eager to hear the Agatha Christie novel you promised to tell me," Alice said as Robert returned to the dining table. "I always enjoyed the tales of Sherlock Holmes and Doctor Watson, but I read all his stories and I couldn't find any more mystery as thrilling as theirs."

"Agatha Christie is a good writer that she was dubbed the Queen of suspense." He adjusted the chair for comfort, "I would tell you what happened in one of her most brilliant novels. The title is "And Then There Were None."

It was Alice turn to adjust the chair. Then she stood up hurriedly. "Wait a minute, let me get some water. I know this would be an interesting one."

Robert smiled as he watched Alice go and get herself a cup of water and she returned.

"Okay shoot."

Robert cleared his throat and he started.

"One early August day, eight people arrive in a small isolated island of Devon. Each of them had an invitation of different circumstance. One, an offer of employment, another, an unexpected late summer holiday, and others had such kinds of invitation. The eight of them arrived one after the other. Thomas and Ethel who are both the workers in the house met them. They told the guests that their hosts, Mr. and Mrs. Owen, had not arrived yet but they left specific instructions to cater for them.

Now, this is where it gets interesting. A framed copy of the nursery rhyme, "Ten little Indians' hangs in every guest's room. Do you know it?

"Yes," an attentive Alice replied.

"Okay... and ten figurines sat on the dining table downstairs. After dinner, a gramophone started playing. It contained a recording that accused each guest of murder but had somehow escaped justice.

Perplexed and befuddled, they started talking. It was then they discovered that none of them knows the host, Mr. Owen. During the discussion, one of them started foaming at the mouth. It was cyanide poisoning. Someone had poisoned him. He died.

Afterwards, they noticed that one of the ten figurines on the dining table was missing and the numbers of figurine equal the number of them alive.

The next morning, another guest died in her sleep. In the afternoon, another guest was dead. The shocking thing was that each of the deaths had so far followed the nursery rhyme. And—

Alice interrupted "Let me guess. The figurines kept reducing with each death."

"Yes. Then the remaining guests decided that they had to search the island. Mr. Owen must be hiding somewhere then coming to kill them one after the other. They had to find him to prevent further deaths. They searched the house and the length and breadth of the Island. They did not see any living thing except the roaring ocean.

When they found nobody on the island, they deduced that one of them must be the killer. By noon the following day, two more guests had died each with a circumstance in the nursery rhyme and a piece of figurine missing each time.

One of them suggested that they searched the rooms, gather all the potentially dangerous items, and lock them up in a room. One of the guests, Lombard who had a gun could not find his gun. One more death and it was a gunshot to the head. By night, the guest found his gun in its original place-someone had replaced it!

One of the guests, a woman, caught a glimpse of someone leaving the house but she lost his trail. She would later discover that one of the remaining guests named, Armstrong, was missing. She told the remaining two guests of her suspicion and they all conclude that Armstrong was the killer. They decided to stay together afterward."

Alice was paying very good attention. The story Robert was narrating was getting interesting by each sentence. She could not wait for the killer to be found and everything to be unrevealed.

"In the morning, they decided to signal an SOS from the island using a mirror and sunlight. It was unsuccessful. One of them decided to return to the house to eat as the two others were hungry. He was killed.

The remaining two were astonished when they found the corpse and they were sure Armstrong was the killer. Before evening, that hypothesis fell apart when Armstrong's body was washed up ashore.

There were now two remaining. Both of them believed each other was the killer. One of them grabbed a gun and in the shuffle, killed the other. The remaining guest, a woman, now went back to the mansion and hung herself.

And then there were none."

Alice was puzzled. What a confusing story. "So who was killing them?"

"Well the killer said he knew the police would never be able to solve the mystery behind the murders, so he would help them. He wrote the solution and kept in inside a bottle, and then he threw it into the ocean.

In the note, he unraveled he was one of the ten invited guests and he had long wished to create an unsolvable puzzle of murders. The ingenious act of the whole novel was that he connived with another guest to fake his death. He said it would allow him to roam freely and find the murderer. He killed the man whom he had connived with. Hence, he was a walking dead, free to roam and execute the murders without any suspicion. He would always run back to lie down where they had laid the corpses.

After he killed everyone, he killed himself. And then there were none."

Alice clapped her hands. "I enjoyed every bit of it, and it was a really puzzling murder. I bet no one in the whole world could figure out the killer except the author herself."

"I quite agree."

"When I get back to Kandersteg, I would rummage the bookshops for her novels like you predicted. You have any more titles for me?"

"Many. But try and look for *The Murder of Roger Ackyrod* and *Murder on the Orient Express.*"

"They all have murders."

"Yes, murder mysteries."

Alice stood up from the chair, yawned and stretched her hands.

"You and Agatha Christie made my night and gave me this lovely feeling. I would sleep with a lovely feeling coursing through my system." She stood and walked to the bed, and then she laid on it, leaving adequate space for Robert. She was soon fast asleep.

Robert was not feeling sleepy yet, so he picked up The Kite Runner and continued reading. After about thirty minutes, he was dozing. After about a dozen jerks, he closed the novel, got up from the chair and he walked to the bed and slept on the space Alice had left for her. He had not slept long when he remembered something. He dropped his legs to the ground and he unbuckled his shoes, then he placed it underneath the bed and he returned to sleep.

They slept in bliss until Alice jerked awake. She was sweating profusely. She turned. Robert was sleeping. He was fully dressed in his suit, and she noticed he was not wearing his shoes.

However, something must have woken her up. She stepped out of bed and moved around the chalet checking for irregularities. She did not find any. She went back to bed.

As soon her back kissed the bed, she heard it. It was a loud noise. Something seemed to hit the side of the chalet. She could hear something that sounded like footsteps.

Was someone trying to break in? A thief? The owner of the chalet?

Gbam! She heard the sound again. Robert was still asleep. This time she had sat upright and she could hear her heart beating fast against her ribcages. Her fingers found the pillow and she held in his a tight embrace.

Gbam! Gbam! Gbam! She tapped Robert and woke him up. This was an emergency. It could as well be a matter of life and death.

Robert woke up. Somnolence was still heavy in his eyes. What could Alice have woken him up for? He had been enjoying the sleep. It was arguably the best since the avalanche. He turned. Alice was holding her pillow tight. She was shivering. As he made to sit up, he heard a sound, Gbam! He could hear footsteps outside. Were they in some sort of cannibal enclave? Or the owner of the chalet. Or- the lights when off.

Darkness started its reign.

The darkness was proof that there was something serious happening out there. In the darkness, Alice found Robert and she locked herself in his embrace. After the darkness had struck, the footsteps stopped, the sound of something hitting the wooden wall of the chalet stopped too. It was all silence.

Then they heard something that sounded like the bleating.

The silence was a relief to Alice but it was not enough for her to release herself from the embrace of Robert. In it, she found comfort and her heartbeats were calm. After about fifteen minutes of silence, she fell asleep.

Robert could not really wrap his head around what has just happened, but he was glad the footsteps had stopped and it was all silent now. It would have been good to go outside and check what caused the disturbance, and particularly the light that went off, but his mind showed him reels of images from the night he had the electric shock from trying to fix the fuse. He gave up before he even tried, and slowly, he lost the battle in trying to keep his eyelids open. He slept in the warm embrace of Alice.

Chapter Seven

They woke up almost together. They had loosened their embrace in the course of sleep. The sun was already up and its rays were filtering in through the window glasses.

Alice remembered what happened in the previous night. She could not imagine what had happened, but she was sure it was okay now. They had to go and open the door and see what caused the noise and power cut the previous night.

After a little hesitation, Robert went out through the window while Alice went to the door to wait until he removed the barrel and open the door. Then she heard a sudden scream. She could feel her heart in her mouth.

Robert!

She ran from the door to the window, stepped on the barrel and took a peep. Robert was alright. His mouth was wide open and held in place with shock. The electrical cable, that supplied the chalet with electricity, had been cut into two.

"Your screams scared me."

Robert looked up. "I am sorry. I was just surprised at what I saw out here."

"Come and open the door and let me see," Alice said, and she returned to the door, waiting for Robert to open it.

Robert opened the door. He and Alice went to the side of the chalet where they had heard the gbam! gbam! Noise and the footsteps. They could see several footprints but they were too small to belong to a human. They followed the trail of the footprints and it led them to the back of the chalet where the electrical cable had been sabotaged.

Alice picked it up and she inspected it. She could see signs of the rubber covering of the wire been gnawed at. She dropped it and started laughing.

"What!" Robert was puzzled. What could be making Alice laugh at a serious matter?

Alice picked up the wire. "I had been suspecting since midnight, but I couldn't just come to a conclusion.'

Robert's face showed it all. The eagerness to know what could have made Alice laughed over the matter at hand.

"Those footprints said it all. They don't belong to a man."

"I agree. They are too small."

"It's good you noticed that too. And you see this wire?" She stretched forth the cable towards him but he did not collect it. He just took a gaze, "It has been gnawed at. Our night hostile visitors were goats! Mountain goats."

Robert's face lit up. Alice's conclusion was so true. He had heard bleating sounds but his fearful state would not allow him to stimulate the scenario in his mind. Goats had taken them for a ride. Robert started laughing and they walked back to the chalet.

This was the third day. Robert suggested they did as they had done the previous day. They should go to the small road. They might get lucky and see a car or another helicopter could whirl pass. Alice agreed to it, but she insisted they eat first.

Robert cleaned the dishes as he had promised the previous night and Alice cooked. They ate, locked up the chalet as they used to do and proceeded to the highway.

When they were passing through the flower field, Alice asked Robert to shed light on something she had been suspecting.

"I noticed you don't like electricity that much."

"Why?" Robert answered, wondering the reason Alice asked the question.

"In the two nights we have stayed here, you have never for once connected the cable to the socket. Even this morning, you didn't collect the wire from me when I told you to observe the gnawing on the wire."

Robert was silent.

"Is there a reason for that? You might as well spill." Alice plucked a flower, "We still have a long way to go."

Robert played dumb for a while, and then he decided to her the whole story. He told her how he was working late and he was the only one in the office, and the lights went out, and his electrician was at the theatre with his laboring wife, and how he searched the fault on Google and he ended up being shocked.

Alice laughed aloud and hard that Robert soon joined him and they were both laughing.

"It's enough to make you develop a phobia. I can only imagine the scenes. But it is funny though."

"It wasn't funny when I ended up spending a week in the hospital for a concussion and electric shock."

Alice made a mental note to do something about it.

Their remaining trip to the road was rather uneventful and boring except for Alice plucking flowers of different species, smelling their fragrance and sometimes tucking them into her hair and asking Robert to look at her if she resembled a girl with a Snapchat flower filter in her head.

Robert, on the other hand, filled himself with hopes on what they would meet when they got to the road.

The small road was at it was the day before. Huge boulders still covered the road. They sat on the log they had used the previous day.

"I hope we get out of her today." Robert expressed his hope.

"I hope too."

"But you don't show that you want to leave here."

"Never judge a man's intention by actions. Some people wear good masks. Like I am doing. If I keep thinking of Kandersteg and how the whole town would not sleep because their golden girl is missing, not to imagine what my parents or siblings would be going through, I would be sick and probably die before we have a chance to be rescued. It is better I try and stay strong for them."

Robert never thought of this. Even though he had come to like Alice within the two days they had spent together, he still felt she was the crazy type and he would never think she wanted to go home. She was right about actions and intention. While so many people think of his success as proof of hard work and passion, it was not. Its fuel was revenge. Revenge aimed at his father-in-law who thought he was a gold digger and his own family who alienated him once he got married to Lucia-particularly Elias, whom he had never imagined would spearhead his family to rebel against him.

"I know we would come through and we would have a success story to tell."

"Definitely. People would be happy to hear how some mountain goats scared the hell out of us."

Alice giggled. "I bet they were hungry. We should leave something outside for them to eat if we get to sleep once more in the chalet."

"I agree. I definitely don't want that kind of hubbub again."

Alice thought of it all. They have been surviving on the savings of someone they never knew; they have been living in his chalet, they even broke his door down and used his resources. They ought to do something about it. So she told Robert.

"You know, we should fix the chalet when we get out of here."

"I never thought of it until you mentioned it. It is not a problem. I would write the owner a check once I get to Zurich."

Alice shook her head. "What if we don't get to meet the owner?"

"Then, I would drop it on a table in the chalet with a note."

"What if another person picks it up or mountain goats get inside and eat it."

"But we would close the door." Robert noticed Alice's face was bland. She was still not satisfied with his answer. "So what do you suggest we do?"

"Good, we replenish his stock, get a carpenter to fix the broken doors, and then you can leave a check and a note as a thank you gesture."

Robert stood. It seemed her heard a noise. He walked back on the asphalted road. He could not see anything, and the sound seemed to have stopped.

"You heard something?"

'It seemed, but now it looks like it was all in my mind."

Alice grinned, and then she returned to her sitting position. Robert returned after spending few more seconds to clear his doubts.

"What would you do when you get back to Zurich?" Alice asked.

Robert was silent for a while. Then he said it. "I would take a small holiday."

"Really!" Alice could not think of Robert without thinking of money, but she had seen it regressed in him form the first time they had met until now.

"These two days I have spent with you, I have seen a side of life I was oblivious to."

"Awww. I am blushing."

"What about you? What will you do when we get rescued?"

"I don't know. Give you a kiss I guess." She watched Robert smile and she gave him a pat on his shoulder and smiled too. "I would probably spend three days being given a prodigal welcome. In those periods, I would narrate how I spent the days and night while I was away. I would probably exaggerate things a bit to make them gasps. I would gladly tell them we fought and won against a mountain lion, and they would not want to believe me until I tell them you are a great hunter who was trained in the hills of Kenya- the Maasai, you know."

Robert had broken into guffaws, and it was slowly overcome by a slight cough which he got rid of and continued laughing. "You are freaking hilarious, you know."

"Then afterward, I will return to my flour shop, but I would need to employ extra hands because I won't be able to contain my crowds of customers who didn't really need to buy flour, but hear bits of the mountain lion tales from my mouth."

"You are a sleuth you know. Like, Hercules Poirot."

"Who is Hercules Poirot?"

"He was one of the sleuths that Agatha Christie used to solve the murder mysteries in her novel."

"That reminds me, I would also get a lot of her novels. How many did she write?"

'Many. About eighty I guess."

Alice opened her mouth and covered it with her right palm in astonishment.

"That is quite some numbers."

Robert stood up and checked something he thought he saw on the horizon. He set his gaze in the direction for a spell, but nothing moved. Dejected, he returned to his seat.

"Let us do a favorite game. I tell you my favorite thing and the reason why I like it."

"Okay."

"What is your favorite color?" Robert asked

"Green."

"Why Green?"

"Because it signifies nature. It is a symbol of peace. It depicts earth in its pristine form." Alice shifted her legs because an ant was crawling past and she did not want to stamp on it. "Now it's your turn."

"What's your favorite movie?"

Robert scratched his head. "I don't do movies. I have not seen one in close to fifteen years now. The last time I went to a cinema was when Lucia once dragged me to see a movie, and it was so boring that I swore to myself to never expose myself to that kind of torture ever again."

"Torture." Alice shook her head. "I am pretty sure you won't have varieties of favorites. Let us play another game."

"Okay, which one?"

"It is called the Truth and Dare game. Whenever is your turn, you announce which of them you intend choosing. Then you either choose to ask me a question, which I must tell the truth about, or dare to do something insane. You choose your own definition of insane."

"It sounds interesting. Let me go first."

"Okay."

"Truth. Are you really thirty-five years old?"

Alice smiled. "Yes, I am. You are invited to come to Kandersteg to see my birth certificate if you want further proof."

"You just don't look thirty-five."

"I don't want to look thirty-five either. My turn. I dare. I dare you to remove your shoe, tie and suit jacket, and you must never wear them today."

Robert's face was covered with red. What was Alice trying to do with the stupid game of hers? Strip him naked. He was not going to do it. It is better they scrap this game right now and forget about anything. They had better invent silence between them while they wait for rescue. On the other hand, taking off his shoe, tie, and the suit would not kill him. His staffs were not here, neither was the public here. Just the two of them. He decided to play along with her to spice up the moment. The red in his face eased off.

He took off his shoes, but still kept his socks. Then unknotted his tie and took off his suit jacket.

Alice started laughing. "You need to look at yourself in the mirror."

The red in Robert's face reappeared. "Were you not the one who dared me?"

"I did, and I dared you to make you look good." She stood and she stretched his hands towards him. "Stand."

Robert stood.

Alice used her hands to unroll Robert's sleeves until they were midway between her palms and elbow, then she untucked his shirts. The next was the socks.

"I wish I had a camera, you would have seen how handsome you look. I bet you have never seen this side to yourself before."

Alice kept looking over his shoulder and rolled sleeves. What does this girl think she is doing. He really liked the rolled sleeve but he had never done so before. The worst was the untucked sleeves. He did feel more comfortable in his groins. His feet kissing the bare ground felt like walking on a lit activated charcoal, but there was a lovely sensation about it that engendered after a few minutes. He stopped trying too hard. Maybe he needed this. Maybe something good would come out of this.

They continued playing the truth and dare game until they grew tired and Alice ended up sleeping on Robert's lap.

They did not see any car or helicopter, so as the sun begun to descend from the sky to its resting place, they decided to return to the chalet and rest for the night. They would continue their search for help the following day.

They were both famished, so quietness crept between them as the trudged past the path and they burst out to the flower fields. As they were about to step onto the path in the field, Alice saw something that invited her curiosity. She stopped, bent and then smiled.

"Do you know this plant?" Alice pointed to a small green plant.

Robert bent and gave it a cursory look. "No, I don't"

Alice folded her right palms and pretended as if she was holding a magic wand. She swung it over the plant several times chanting in incoherent language. Then she stopped. "Touch the plant. It has been hexed by my magic."

Robert touched the plant and to his amazement, its leaves folded inwards. An involuntary action drew his fingers away.

"Watch closely, it would open again." Alice continued the imaginary wand thing and the incoherent speaking then she stopped. The plants had opened its leaves again.

Robert could not believe it. Alice was a magician! No wonder how she had been doing all she was doing. He had always doubted her abilities. It was only a superhuman:

who would hear an avalanche coming, who would fix electrical cable without fear, who would deduce goats were what caused the disturbance the other night.

He touched the plant once again and it folded inward again. Robert stood. His face was flooded with astonishment.

Alice wanted to play him and never reveal to him the plant acted naturally but the reactions she was seeing from him made her change her decision.

"Shameplant, that's the name."

"Which name?"

"The plant I told you to touch. There is no magic about it."

"No magic."

"Yes. It does that to prevent itself from harm. The only magic is in your face." She touched Robert soft cheeks, stood on her toes, and started moving her pouted lips towards Robert's.

Robert saw Alice's pouted lips coming towards her. He looked into her eyes and all he could see was a glistening light. He craned his neck and met her halfway. Her lips were luscious and tasted like chocolate.

Alice ran her hands through the button of Robert's long sleeves shirt, took it off his body to reveal a well-chiseled athletic body. This was the first time she saw his bare chest. She ran her palms around his body as love waves vibrated into her body.

Robert had allowed Alice to remove his shirt. It was now time for him to remove her blouse. They broke the mouth connection while he helped her remove her blouse. Then they continued kissing while his hands went to her back where he intended to find the hook of her brassiere. It was bare!

"It is a front opener." Alice managed to say.

"What?"

"It opens from the front."

Robert withdrew his hands to the front where the hook was supposed to be. Just at the middle of her cleavage. He unhooked the brassiere and he helped her took it off, all still while kissing.

He allowed Alice to caress his body for a spell, and then he took control as he fondled her breasts with his hands in a gentle, yet sensuous way.

Alice was already moaning by this time. Then they fell on the flowers.

Robert undid his zips and his male hardness escaped from the cloth prison it had been. He pressed it into her and she moaned with pleasure. She moved closer to him, grinding her hips against his, and then he felt heating growing in his loins.

She stroked him gently and the excitement they both felt knew no bounds. They fell into the flowers separated from each other and they watched the sun dying out. Alice wished they could watch it close its doors while the stars open theirs, but they had things they had to take care of.

'We should get going," Alice sat, picked her brassiere and started to wear it.

"We don't have to hurry; we can spend the night here," Robert said in a tinged voice as he pulled Alice's arm to rejoin him in the flowers.

"We should stay here so that goat friends can come and ram us with their horns right." She was wearing her blouse.

On hearing 'goats' his mind replayed the fearful ordeal they had suffered at the hands of mountain goats the previous nights and how they destroyed the cable supplying electricity to the chalet. Now they had to repair the wire. He did not know if there was food remaining in the chalet. They might have to go to the *mazot* to get some food and water for the night and probably the next morning. The sun would soon set and it would be darkness afterward. All these made Robert jump from the flowers and started wearing his clothing.

They walked to the chalet in silence, each of them still relishing the dose of excitement they had derived from exploring each other's body.

It was getting dark by the time they got to the chalet. Alice suggested they repaired the gnawed wire first, and then they would go to the *mazot*, get some food and water then return to the chalet.

"Why not go on with the repairs. It is really nothing. You just connect both naked ends of the wire. Let me go and take stock and see what we need." Alice went into the chalet while she left Robert to go to the back and reconnect the wire.

They had little rice and spaghetti remaining, but it would not be sufficient for the night and the following morning. They had better get some more. She took a mental note of what they needed and she went to the back to meet Robert who should have been through with the reconnection of wire.

To her amazement, Robert had not done anything. His face gave him off. He was scared!

Alice smiled. She could see he was shivering and he was not even holding the wires.

“It is time to kill your electricity fears.” Alice flashed a smile at him. “The basic safety of electricity is that you don’t allow your hands to touch the mains.”

“And how do you know the mains?”

“You don’t always know, but there is a way we can guarantee an overall safety.” She pulled his hands and they went to the solar panel installation. The wires from the solar panel went into a small shed that housed an inverter and battery.

“I don’t know how these things work, but I know if you remove this fuse, electricity will not flow through again.” She removed the fuse.

Fear filled Robert up that he closed his eyes while Alice removed the fuse. He thought she would be shocked as he was shocked the other night, but to his surprise, nothing happened to Alice. She was now placing the fuse on one of the battery. Then it came back to him the reason why he was shocked. He had inserted his bare hands into the fuse hole where the mains where.

Alice led him back to where the gnawed wires were.

“Now, we can work with our bare hands without fears that we would be shocked. “ She picked up a wire and passed it to Robert, “Hold it, it can’t shock you.”

Robert was scared at first, but the sight of Alice holding the other wire calmed his fears and he collected it. Alice worked with her teeth and she peeled the rubber from the edge of the wire she was holding. She beckoned to Robert to do the same. He did with a leap of faith and once again, he was surprised he was not shocked. Maybe he had been overprotective of himself.

He gave the peeled wire to Alice and she connected them together. Then she went to the chalet and she returned with nylon in which she used to wrap the exposed part of the wire. Afterwards, she connected it to the socket at the back of the chalet.

"Now, we only need to fuse and there shall be light," Alice said as she walked to the solar panel installation.

When they got to the installation, Alice picked up the fuse she was about to fix it back to its position when she heard Robert's voice.

"Let me do it."

Alice gave him the fuse and she stepped aside so that he could have all the space to himself.

Robert collected the fuse and he approached the installations. He was about to replace it when his hands froze mind air. The images flashed through his mind: the concussion, the hospital with the disinfectant smell, the spirals, and the throbbing headaches.

"Just replace it. Nothing would happen to me, trust me." Alice's voice rang out giving him a push.

He closed his eyes and he replaced the fuse in a slow motion. The connection clicked. There was a small spark and Robert removed his hands in haste. He turned; saw Alice's smile and a lit chalet. His fear of electricity was finally conquered.

They left the solar panel installation and went to get the food and water they needed from the *mazot* before it became fully dark. Soon, they were back at the chalet with the food and water they fetched.

Alice was cooking and for the first time since the avalanche, Robert was helping her with the cooking.

"I have this strange feeling this would be our last night here," Robert said, putting some rice in a bowl.

"And when did you become a seer? This isn't stock market or anything o."

"I know. But I just have the feeling." He added water to the rice.

"Add four more handful of rice to it."

"Won't it be too much?"

"Let me worry about that aspect."

They put the rice on fire while they went to sit on the dining table while the rice was cooking.

"So Mr. Seer, you said we would leave here tomorrow. Have you called someone?"

"Call? Don't you remember your phone is dead?"

"Now, that reminds me." Alice stood from the chair. "I have not seen my phone in a while."

"It is not in your bag?"

"My bag is in the car. I tucked the phone into my pocket after you returned it." She felt the front and back pockets of her jeans pants but they were flat. "But I can't find it now." Her face had contoured into helplessness. She started shifting the chairs at the dining table to check underneath them.

Robert got himself involved in the search. They started at the table opposite the fireplace, and then he moved to the bed area. He lifted the bed at one edge and checked underneath. "Look what I found," He said, still holding up thc bcd.

Alice came running forth and she found it. Her phone was lying underneath the bed and something else was beside it. It did not pique Alice interest because she could not think of something to do with it. It was a pen.

She bent and picked her phone but she neglected the pen.

"Help me pick that pen." Robert requested, pointing to the pen.

Now, she picked the pen and Robert dropped the bed afterward. Dinner was soon ready and Alice served them. They ate in almost silence except for the sound of the cutleries hitting the dishes and teeth.

When they were though and they had packed the plates aside, Alice took the remaining rice outside the chalet and she poured it on the ground where the goats were most active the other night.

Robert wanted Alice to tell him a story, but Alice told him she needed rest and that she would tell him when they were heading to the road the following day. Alice went to bed. Robert tried to read the last part of The Kite Runner where Amir discovered Hassan's son, and he took him kite running. It was the best part of the book for him the first time he had read it and the emotional delight he experienced from reading was without no match ever since. He hoped to be able to recreate those delightful emotions tonight but as he tried, Alice's face kept flashing on the page.

He closed his eyes and tried to fight it. Still yet, the flashes kept coming. Resigned to his mental emotions, he went to bed, unbuckled his shoe and lay on the bed. At first, he lay on his side of the bed but there was this pain in his groin.

An erection!

He extended his leg thigh around Alice's hips. He heard her giggle and she turned, her face beaming with a smile. Then she stretched her mouth towards his and they continued from where they stopped at the flower field.

When they got to the zenith of excitement, they both fell back to their respective sides of the bed and slept off.

Chapter Eight

They woke up almost the same time. They both yawned in unison and their outstretched arms even touched each other.

"Good morning." Robert greeted as he took his legs off the bed and started wearing his shoe.

"Morning. It was my best night in a long time."Alice replied.

"Me too."

"And the goats didn't disturb. It seemed your food trick did work."

"It did." Alice yawned once more and she got out of bed.

Robert opened the door and Alice took the plates they had used the previous night outside. The next thing she did was to check the food she had poured at the side of the chalet. The goats ate them all. She returned to clean the dishes while Robert returned to the chalet and set to work with the pen he had found the previous night.

When Alice returned the washed dishes to the table beside the fireplace, she met Robert smiling.

"Look at what I have written for the owner." He passed the paper on which he had written on to Alice.

She collected it and read.

'For two days and three nights, this chalet housed the inception, gestation, and delivery of a time indelible friendship. I would be eternally grateful for you Mr. … (Pardon me for not knowing your name) for building this chalet at this particular spot

We broke the door and that of the mazot, both which we promise to fix. Also, we used some of the food supplies therein, which we also promise to replenish.

You may never know how grateful we are to you. Without your chalet and its supplies, we might have been dead by now. With all our hearts, we are very grateful for your help.

Robert and Alice

PS: your chalet also helped me to cure my phobia of electricity.

You can get me on 079 835 57 14

"Should I also write it from my viewpoint and tell him that he should keep his chalet clean and void of dust the next time?" Alice said in a sarcastic voice.

Robert could not help but laugh at her question.

"So Seer, I can see you are physically and mentally prepared to leave, and you have the right amount of hope." Alice continued.

"Well, I had not always relied on hope. You taught me what kind of thing hope is."

"Okay. Keep hunting me with my words."

They boiled some spaghetti, ate them and cleaned the plates. Then they cleaned the chalet. Robert placed the note on the table opposite the fireplace and he kept the pen on top. Then they exited the chalet.

Robert had carried the wood to cover the entrance and he was about to start rolling the barrel when Alice remembered something.

"Please, I forgot something. I need to pick it."

Robert carried the wood away from the doorframe and he looked towards the field. Alice went into the chalet and within twenty seconds, she came out. Robert secured the door, closed the window and disconnected the electric cable from the socket. They were good to go.

They held each other's hand and they started walking through the flowers. Then they heard it.

A helicopter!

They ran as they did when they were trying to escape the avalanche. When they got to the flower field, they could see the helicopter. It was painted white but its tail and underneath was painted red. Alice recognized the organization. The Air-Glacier emergency service that rescues people from glaciers and mountain related dangers. It was going in the direction of the place where the avalanche came down.

Alice removed her blouse while Robert took off his suit and they began to wave it at the helicopter and accompany it with shouts. The helicopter did not stop. They kept on running. They ran past the flower field and the path in the forest until the burst out onto the road.

They could hear the cacophony of noise. Car engines, the voice of people and the rotor noise from the helicopter were the few they could recognize.

They were going to be rescued!

By the time they came of the bend towards the portion of the road in which the boulders had fallen unto, their excitement knew no bounds.

There was a Caterpillar bulldozer and excavator on the ground to lift the boulders and there was a dump truck on the ground that could lift the boulders away. There were many members of the Swiss emergency service on the ground and many reporters with cameramen.

Robert and Alice approached them and they declared their identity. The medical team examined them even though they told them they were alright.

When the boulders were lifted, Robert and Alice laughed at the sight of their cars. It was no different from the crushed cars in a scrap yard.

After certificating that both of them were alright, they declared both of them free to go home. The reporters crowded them and pelted questions from every angle. After answering a question from about four reporters, a police officer shielded them away from the restless reporters.

The police officer told them they would use a helicopter to carry Robert to Zurich while a bus would carry Alice to Kandersteg. They were to leave immediately.

Robert never imagined his rescue would be filled with so much emotion. He had enjoyed the three days with Alice and he had learned the valuable lesson he might have never been able to learn if the avalanche had not happened.

"I will miss you." He said. It was apparent in his voice that he was on the verge of crying. He was only holding them.

After the second day, Alice knew she would miss Robert whenever they were to depart. It had been fun-filled three days, one that would cling to her memory forever.

She did not reply to Robert. She only beckoned to Robert to call her.

Robert was about to enter the helicopter when he remembered he did not have Alice phone number. She turned back and chased after Alice.

"Can you believe that I don't have your phone number?"

"What!" Alice hit her head with her balled palm. It was true. They never exchanged phone numbers. She sent her eyes on a search and she found a pen at the breast pocket of the police officer that was accompanying her to the bus that would take her home. She borrowed the pen from her then she wrote her number on Robert's palm.

Robert planted a kiss on her forehead and he returned to his waiting helicopter fighting a huge urge to turn back as he went. He won.

Chapter Nine

The first thing Robert did as soon as he got off the Air-Glacier helicopter when it landed in Zurich was to instruct Mr. Barkley to get a handyman, a carpenter, and an electrician and go to the chalet for repairs and to replenish the supply at the *mazot*. Then he got on to his work properly.

He was amazed that the deal with Mr. Ocean did go on as planned!

How come?

Mr.Barkley was not around because he had followed the workers to ensure the work was completed in haste. He sent his mind on a rummaging mission on how it was possible, but he was not able to unravel it.

He gathered and asked his staffs how the deal was pulled off. None of them knew how. They just knew the deal had been signed!

Such a mystery

When Mr. Barkley returned from the chalet with picture proofs that the repairs were done and efficient, he came clean on the whole case. He was the mole!

For the moment, Robert felt the saliva in his tongue dry off, his brains felt like they were floating, his heartbeat skipped and his fingers trembled.

His most loyal worker was actually a mole!

It was afterward that Barkley explained everything. He told him how Weinstein and sons holdings had capitalized on his dark side and used it to blackmail him.

He came home drunk one night to meet his door jimmied and a corpse whose clothes were stained with patches of blood and a bloodstained knife was lying on the floor. Not long after that, the CEO of Weinstein and sons holding, Mr. Reese, walked in with cameramen. They captured the whole scene. Then he told him they had been watching him for a long time. They had taken several fingerprint samples from him and they had used it to smear the knife lying on the floor.

When forensic get to the scene, all evidence will point to Barkley as the murderer. The court would follow the evidence rather than his innocent claiming testimony. He would spend time behind bars for it. His career would be dead as soon as the police and reporters arrive. His wife and daughter, who were on vacation, would hate him for it. His friends would desert him and he would probably die in prison.

He had a chance to redeem himself. He would act as a mole. They would tap his phone and email. If he tried to tell the authorities or Robert, the evidence would be released and he would be doomed.

Barkley had no choice. He had to concur. So in line with the blackmail, he employed the help of, Michael, a computer hacker, which was provided by Mr. Reese, and he came into the company building under the guise of a computer technician and hacked into Robert's phone and personal computers. Through that, he had knowledge of all business deals before they were hatched to the staffs.

When the thirty-five million dollars deal with Mr. Ocean came through, he knew instantly that he would not relay that business deal to the Weinsteins. Of recent, their business deals were snatched by competitors and they had done very little deals. If Robert did not get the deal with Mr. Ocean, by the following month, they would not be able to pay the salaries of the companies' staff.

Of what benefit would that be to him? It was not as if Mr. Reese would employ him or something.

He had to keep the information secret.

He already knew Robert was going to pick Mr. Ocean at the airport. A day before Mr. Ocean was to land in Zurich; Robert had gone to the Swiss Alps to make a personal vacation preparation for Mr. Ocean. He was doing this all in the name of playing with his cards close to his chest.

When Robert did not arrive and his calls to his phone did not go through, Barkley knew there was trouble. It was more serious when Robert called with him a strange number but he could not hear him clearly. He called the number as soon as the call disconnected but it never patched through.

It was then Barkley decided to replace Robert and pick up Mr. Ocean from the airport. Armed with the files and information he had gotten from hacking Robert's calls and emails, he had enough information to act as a vicegerent. And it worked like magic. Mr. Ocean signed.

Robert did not know if he should be angry with Barkley for not telling him all these earlier or he should cry out for his incredible luck.

He reclined on his cushion chair, placed his legs on his worktable and he smiled.

"That girl is a seer!"

Alice quote from The Shawshank Redemption came to him. '*Hope is a good thing, maybe the best of things and no good thing ever dies.*'

He returned his legs to the floor and picked up his phone. Then he remembered Barkley was still in front of him.

"I am mad at you, and at the same time, I am happy. Take the day off, tomorrow, we would talk about your pay rise, how to nail that Reese bastard and your special bonus for the deal you pulled."

"Thank you," an ecstatic Barkley said as he swiveled and went out of the office dancing on his toes.

Robert opened his palms as soon as Barkley left the office. Alice number was still there. He started in putting it on his phone until he reached the last number. It had washed off!

Damn!

He took out a paper and wrote out the ten possible numbers it could be then he started trying them one after the other. Not one worked. He searched the Internet for a flower show in Kandersteg run by an "Alice", but he could not find anything…

+++

Alice knew she would have a grand welcome whenever she got home and it panned out as she had told Robert. She even got to the part where she told Julian and her other inquisitive siblings that she and Robert fought and won against a mountain Lion.

The story surprised them and they asked for more.

"I am sure the Mountain Lions came back and your Maasai friend killed them with his bare hands like Samson in the Bible." Her youngest sister said.

"Yes, Robert once lived amongst the Maasai, but that doesn't mean he can kill a Lion with his bare hands."

"Then how did he kill it? You were there."

"Yes, I was. We—j" her phone rang.

"Hello, seer."

She recognized Robert's voice. "No, you are the seer. Remember you predicted that we would be rescued. And it came to pass."

"That is true, but you talked about hope and my business deal with Mr. Ocean."

"What about it?"

'I won the deal!" he screamed.

Alice felt excitement flooding all over her. How was it possible? She had been preaching hope alright but she didn't imagine the deal would pull through particularly when he made it clear the deal was hinged on giving Mr. Ocean a good reception from the airport.

"How did it happen?"

Robert narrated everything to her. How Barkley turned out to be the mole he had always been suspecting and it ended up being a blessing in disguise for him.

"Your story has made me have more believe in hope," Alice confessed.

“Even me too. I will watch the Shawshank Redemption on Netflix tonight. It would be the first time I would do so in-“

“Fifteen years.” Alice completed it for him.

They both laughed afterward.

“My siblings are here and they are asking me about the man who fought mountain Lions with his bare hands. Would you do them the pleasure of telling them how you did it?”

Robert giggled, “Are you serious now?”

Alice took her mouth away from the phone and faced her siblings, “I have the man who fought with the Lions on the phone. You want to hear him talk?” Then she removed the phone from cheek and stretched it towards her siblings who were now chorusing “Yessss.”

Then she replaced the phone to her cheek. “So I hope you can hear them.”

“You are something else Alice. More than crazy.”

“My siblings are waiting.”

“Okay, I would cook something up. But I promise you, I am not the best of storytellers.”

“I didn’t tell them you are Aesop.”

Robert laughed. “Okay, I am ready.”

Alice removed the phone from her cheek; put it on speaker mode and she gave her phone to Julian. Then she left them in their attentive mode as the listened to Robert as he spun a tale from the hills of Kenya to the cow blood drinking culture of the Maasai and then the chalet in the middle of nowhere and the disturbing mountain Lions.

Chapter Ten

+++

Two months later

+++

The CEO of Weinstein and sons holdings, Mr. Reese, ended up in prison. Barkley had reported the police about the blackmail and with testimony from Michael, the computer hacker, and further investigations, Barkley was let off the blackmail noose. Michael was hired to be part of the IT team.

Life continued without a fuss.

Robert was sitting in his office and he was having problems opening a file, so he called Barkley and told him about it. He tried it was also not able to log in, so he in turn called Michael.

Michael came over and troubleshot the laptop. After few minutes, he came up with the breaking news. The laptop had been infected by a Trojan virus!

"How come?" Barkley blurted out, "I thought you just installed new anti-virus last week."

'Yes, my team did for all the desktops and laptops here," then he got thinking. He started checking for the anti-virus on Robert's laptop.

"What! It is out of date… but!"

"Don't fret it," Robert said, realizing the mistake he had made. "One of your team members came for the upgrade thing sometimes last week but I was so busy that I told him not to worry at the moment."

"But he should have come back.' Barkley said. His hands were already balled and his brows were furrowed together.

"I am sure he did come back. But remember I traveled and I am just returning."

"That's true."

"So, what do we do now?"

"Let me check the extent of the virus." He started pressing the keyboard of the laptop while Robert and Barkley watched. "Did you by any chance connect any external device to this laptop between last week and today?"

"Yes, I did use the flash drive to check the proposal Barkley had written and I copied it on my phone."

"Damn!" Michael slammed his hands on the table. We need to format the laptop, your phone and the flash drive.

Robert shook his head. "I will be losing a lot of files."

"I thought you use Google drive to backup your files?"

"That's true. I use it for important files."

"I think that is better than losing out on everything."

Michael was still pressing the keypads of the laptop then he discovered something. "Let me have your phone." He asked from Robert.

Robert gave it to him.

He ran some checks on it.

"Oops. This is compromised."

"What do you mean? Please explain further."

"It is a fact that your laptop was infected with a Trojan virus. But then, it shouldn't be because you didn't use antivirus for a week. There are several computers all over the world without antivirus and they work just fine. Then that led me to think there might be a bug in the laptop.

So I checked. It appeared that someone has hacked your laptop and phone."

"Again!" Robert screamed.

"The hacker must be stealing information from us. What are we going to do? You once hacked this company remember."

"I have figured it out. We need to format the laptop and sire; you need to change your phone number. It is compromised."

"Okay do it. Do it now." Robert ordered. "Do whatever you have to do to stop this hacker."

Michael did his work, he formatted the laptop, and he decommissioned the phone.

Chapter Eleven

Alice was going to her flour shop when she stopped at the newsstand stand to catch a glimpse of the news headlines. To her utmost surprise, she found a feature article on Tell! Magazine. It was about Robert and her and how they survived the three days of being trapped. A Lisa Blankett wrote the article.

Alice could not remember giving an interview but she did remember. It did not look like an interview. Lisa Blankett had gone to interview Robert in Zurich but she was not able to because of his busy schedule. Lisa took it upon herself to look for Alice in Kandersteg. She roamed Kandersteg until she was tired and she decided to take a rest in the awnings of Alice's shop. That was when she met her.

Lisa did stay with Alice for two days in which she divulged all the memories of her three days with Robert in the chalet. She had misplaced Lisa's contact afterward and they fell out of touch.

She bought the magazine and brought out her phone. She fiddled her hands with the contacts and Robert's number. She dialed it but it did not go through.

The same custom voice that the number is out of service. She had been getting such replies lately.

What Alice did not know was while the hacker in Robert's office had been beaten at his own game and shown the exit door, so was Alice's contact because her number was deleted alongside the other stuff.

That's it?

The story ends here? No real love story has such a cheesy and unrealistic ending! Even if Robert lost Alice's phone number he could have driven up to Kandersteg to see her. Unfortunately this is life! One second to early or one second late and the complete path of our life's change.

Robert wanted to go to Kandersteg on the same day. But as usual overloaded with his work, he planned it for the next day, the next week, the next month, arriving at the point of such a big shame that he was afraid to meet Alice. The point of non-return was reached.

Alice tried to call Robert a few times, but as there was no answer she gave up. She realized that the "Hollywood" love stories do not exist in real life.

… but the path of life continuous….

Chapter Twelve

+++

Winter

+++

Mr. Wayne was a native of England but he stopped spending the winter there since the age of thirty-five. He preferred the mountain air of Switzerland to the crowded streets of London, Manchester or Liverpool.

He liked the mountain air because it refreshed his ideas. You see, Mr. Wayne was a novelist. He wrote under the pseudo-name, Mr. DouByou. He wrote crime and military thrillers and his novels were usually No 1 on the New York Times Bestseller. He had been compared to Robert Ludlum and Tom Clancy. The plots of his novels were usually woven intricately that a magazine once placed his IQ somewhere between 170 and 200.

What they do not know was that Mr. Wayne took a visit every winter to thė Swiss mountains. He had his chalet by the small road where he spends the whole winter. He was usually alone but there was nothing to worry about because food and his favorite filtered cigarettes were stocked in the chalet.

He would dwell on the silence and he would write out his outlines, flesh them up, sometimes tearing the unsatisfied pages out and rewrite them. By the time the winter months are over, he would have finished both the first and second draft and he would turn them into his editor by the time he returned to London.

But now, this was Mr. Wayne's last trip to the mountains. He was going to write what might be his last novel.

He turned his BMX power bike off from the road through the path in the forest. He would not know that a few months ago, a man and a woman were running down the same path to save themselves.

Mr. Wayne thought of his will. He had everything sorted out. Ninety percent of his properties were to be given out to charity, while nine percent went to his wife and adopted a child. He thought of giving Williams, his nephew, the writing chalet, but of recent, he had started to misbehave. He flunked classes at school and had was even sent to the Juvenile home of recent for robbing a grocery store with his group of friends.

Wayne turned his power bike towards the flower field. He did not deserve it. Nevertheless, maybe he should give him anyways. He hoped Williams could make good use of it. There was no reason to think about his matter too much. He should rather focus his thought on writing his novel and having the best time of his life.

He stopped the power bike in the front of the chalet. It appeared different. The front door looked new like someone just changed it in recent. He dismounted the bike and walked to the door. To his surprise, there was a brand new key hanging on a piece of nail that had been driven into the door.

New keys? Some family surprise?

He took the keys and he inserted it into the keyhole with mixed fillings. As he opened the door and the trapped air fell on his face, he knew the chalet had had a visitor.

As he entered, his gaze picked up a piece of paper with a pen on top. He walked towards it and picked it up then he read.

Wayne figured that two persons wrote the letter because the handwriting towards the end was different.

A deluge of excitement flooded him. He had never imagined the chalet could do help to any other person apart from himself. He smiled, sat and fished out his phone then he called his lawyer.

"I have an adjustment to make in my will."

+++

Alice was almost home from her shop when she met Julian walking towards her direction.

"Sup bro." She spoke to him from a distance.

"I want to get to Angela's house. I want to borrow one of his PlayStation pads. Mine is faulty." He was already by her side by the time he completed his sentence.

"Okay, you should go then. Don't stay long."

Julian had walked past her when he remembered something. "A letter came in for you from Bern."

"Bern? I don't know anyone in Bern."

"Well, maybe you won a lottery there." He chuckled, and then he turned and continued walking.

Bern. She had never been there and she never had a friend who lived in Bern. On the other hand, maybe an old friend of hers had moved to Bern and she was writing to her from there. This was unlikely because all the friends she ever had were in Kandersteg. The only exception to this was Robert. Well, his number stopped going through and he never reached out to her. Even at that, Robert lived in Zurich and she could not think of a reason why he would decide to move to Bern. She decided to sum all her thoughts to what the content of the letter was and who sent it.

The first thing she did when she got home was to go and find the letter. She found it where new letters were filed.

It was indeed addressed to her from a Bern address.

Who could it be?

She opened the letter and read through. It was a lawyer who told her she was a beneficiary of Mr. Wayne's will, and she should come the following Monday. Enclosed in the letter was a train ticket with a promise that there would be a taxi available to bring her to the lawyer's office.

It was strange, but her curiosity would not let her allow it go. She decided that she would prepare to go to the lawyer's office the following Monday.

+++

Robert was rounding up for the day when his secretary brought a letter.

"You have a letter from Bern."

"Bern!"

"Yes."

"Let me see." Robert stretched his hands and collected the letter. He perused the envelope. It was addressed to him and it had a Bern address. He tore the envelop open. "You may leave.'

His secretary walked out of the room while he rested his back and started reading. It was from a lawyer in Bern. He said he was a beneficiary of a will and that he should come the following Monday to claim it. He had enclosed a train ticket and promised a taxi would be available to see pick him up.

He picked his phone and called his lawyer. Then he explained the latter to him. His lawyer told him not to fret but go to the lawyer's office in Bern.

Robert decided he would put Barkley in-charge on Monday while he went to Bern.

Chapter Thirteen

+++

Monday, Bern Main Train Station

11:30am

+++

Alice had a mixed feeling as soon as the train arrived at the main station. Would the taxi be waiting as promised? The letter had promised the taxi would be waiting at since 11:00 am, thirty minutes before the train arrived, so she was never going to miss it.

The promise was bold but she felt it would have been convenient if the lawyer had included his phone number. That way, he would be able to call him should in case the taxi does not show up.

As she walked through the entrance hall towards the exit, she saw a man raising a placard with her name on it.

She approached him.

"I am Alice." She opened the handbag for identification. "The lawyer sent you?"

The man nodded his head. "This way," He beckoned after he had seen her identification.

He led her to a taxi parked at the curb of the train station entrance. He opened the door for her and held it while she entered, then he went to the front, entered and started driving.

"We go straight to the lawyer."

+++

11:40am

+++

Robert was not troubled. His lawyer had assured him the letter was genuine. On a normal day, he would have neglected it, but he was less busy and there was something in his curious mind that kept pushing him to go to Bern.

He found a man holding a placard with his name written on top. He approached him, confirmed it was the right Robert and they set on the journey to the lawyer's chambers.

+++

When the taxi driver stopped Alice in front of the lawyer's chamber and beckoned the stairs to her, she still felt uneasy. As she climbed the stairs, she told herself,

'If you can survive three days with a complete stranger, why should a few minutes with a stranger in a more open place frighten you?"

She opened the door and a smiling young receptionist whom Alice reckoned would be a junior lawyer welcomed her. He ushered her into the main office of the lawyer.

The man she met had fair complexioned, freckles littered, oval-shaped, face, and he was holding a cup of something steamy. Coffee maybe. He was wearing a white suit, which was in great contrast to the black suit Alice had developed in mind.

"Have your seat." He offered, pointing to one of the two shirts opposite him.

Alice sat down. Her gaze went to the office and she caught a glimpse of hung certificates and by her right, long glassed shelf that housed several books. They could possibly be up to two hundred books in there.

She returned her gaze and set it on the freckled face of the lawyer.

"I got this letter." She opened her bag and brought it out.

"No need to show me, I sent them." He dropped the cup in his hands to the table.

"Why? How? I don't know you from anywhere." She accompanied it with a contoured face.

"I never knew you too until my client called me and told me to track you."

"Who is your client?"

"Mr. Wayne."

"I don't know any Mr. Wayne."

"Sorry. Not many people know him by that. He is popularly called Mr. DouByou."

"Mr. DouByou!" Her eyes were bulging. "I know him. I have read couples of his novels."

"That's true."

"But wait. How did Mr DouByou know me?"

"Well, it is a simple story you would connect to. Let us wait for the other beneficiary. He will soon be here and I will tell you together."

He picked up his phone and called someone. After enquiring where the person was, he said 'okay' and he dropped the call.

"They are just around the corner."

Alice's mind ran wild. Mr. DouByou. How? Did she enter for a raffle in his novels? No, she could not remember any. The only raffle she entered and did not win was that of James Pink, the romance writer, she had lost interest in any raffle because she did not win.

Although it started sounding like a joke but the circumstances that surrounded it looked serious.

The door opened. Alice turned her head. The receptionist was ushering in a man wearing a sports face cap, dark-tinned eyeglasses, a casual Tank top and cargo short. His legs were hairy and they saddled on a white trainer.

He sat on the empty chair beside Alice before the lawyer even before said anything.

"Can I get a cup of coffee?" the man requested.

Alice looked at him. He seemed rude. She decided to mind her business and face what Mr. DouByou had with her.

+++

Robert looked at the girl beside him. She wore those long wigs these new generation girls wear. The wig covered the side of her face and she was even looking front. She seemed too serious because he could not see a cup of steaming coffee in front of her. He wondered what she had come to do in the office. Alternatively, maybe she was a junior lawyer.

Robert fished out a letter from his pocket and he stretched it forth towards the lawyer. "I got this from you."

"Yes, I was going to explain it all to her, but I wanted you to be around so that I won't have to repeat myself since it is a matter that concerns both of you.

"Both of us." Robert and the woman said in unison and he turned to look at her. Unable to recognize the stranger, he turned back to the lawyer, his eyes probing for answers.

+++

The lawyer opened a file and brought out a document.

"I would like you both to listen attentively; I will tell you the whole story."

His clients nodded.

"Some months ago, my client called me at the start of winter. He said he wanted an alteration to his will. There would be two new beneficiaries and he had never met them before. I was surprised, but I still have to do my client's bidding nevertheless. He told me he got hold of their addresses. That was how I was able to track you."

He paused and opened the file again. This time, he brought out a paper. It was old and it had words written on it.

"Apparently, both of you wrote this." He passed it towards the woman.

+++

Alice received the paper from the lawyer. She had never imagined that she would see it again! The letter Robert had written when they were leaving the chalet. Wait! Was it Robert sitting beside her?

She turned and looked at him again. The shape of the face does resemble Robert's. But, a tank top and cargo shorts! It could not be Robert. She decided to take a bold step, so she stretched her hands and removed his eyeglasses. Fear initially overrode her of the expectation but behold, Robert was staring at her!

+++

Robert had noticed the way the woman's face changed as soon she started reading the paper the lawyer gave her. When she removed his eyeglasses, his mind plunged into a fiery mode and he was about to attack her when he heard her scream his name. "Robert!"

She stood and gave him a tight embrace. Robert was still trying to place the voice. It does sound familiar but he could not place the face.

The woman released him from her embrace. "You don't remember me. Alice?" She stretched the paper towards him. He collected it, still dazed. As soon as he read the first two sentences, the memories came back flooding.

For two days and three nights, this chalet housed the inception, gestation, and delivery of a time indelible friendship. I would be eternally grateful for you Mr … (Pardon me for not knowing your name) for building this chalet at this particular spot

It was his turn to scream 'Alice' and hold her tight in his embrace. She had changed so much. The last time he saw her, when he was leaving in the Air-Glacier helicopter, he remembered how her face looked. Heart shaped with no makeup and an auburn hair. But this was a black wig. No wonder why he had missed her.

They spent the next few minutes talking about how they lost other's contact.

+++

The lawyer had been watching them for a while then he decided it was time to go official again so that he could attend the meeting he had at 3pm.

He tapped his hands on the table and it caught their attention.

"Before you came in, I told her both of you are beneficiaries of Mr. DouByou's will. He found that in his writing chalet and he decided to will it to both you since it meant a lot to you. And he also ordered that brand new Bentleys be given to each of you."

"What!" They both screamed.

"Where is he now?" Alice asked.

"He was diagnosed with Stage Three Lung Cancer. He died in the summer."

The lawyer watched both of their faces fall. He opened a file and the brought out a document.

"If you will both sign here," He pointed to a spot. "This will transfer the chalet's ownership from Mr.DouByou you to both of you."

While both of them signed.

His phone ranged. It was his secretary. He spoke a while on the phone. "Okay, thank you." He brought out a hand-over document and placed it before them. "My secretary just told me your cars are ready. You will need to sign this."

They had signed the document.

Robert and Alice were brimming with a smile by the time they left the lawyer's office.

"So what are your travel plans?" Alice asked, as they were given the keys to their respective Bentleys.

"I think you know what I have in mind."

"I don't know what you have in mind. You have changed greatly from the last time I saw you. You are wearing Tank shirt and cargo shorts in place of a suit. Damn!"

"Well, you made me change. Madam Hope."

Alice giggled.

"Well, I think we should—"

'Let me complete it," Robert said, "We should visit the chalet."

Alice gave him a hi-five and they got into their respective cars.

They drove off; Robert was in front while Alice was following closely behind.

Robert was driving his black Bentley up the Swiss Alps. Even though the ambient air was cold and there was a thunderstorm coming, he decided against sliding down the windows. Instead, he switched on the artificial air conditioning of the car. It was blowing cold and he loved it that way.

Alice was driving her black Bentley up the Swiss Alps and she was at an average speed of 100km/hr. She had wound down her car window so that the cold mountain zephyr would blow inside. She wished to drive faster but the man in front is as slow as a snail.

She placed her hand on the horn and blew it many times. Then the driver rolled his car to a halt and came out.

Alice came out too.

"You own a Bentley but you drive it like a Citroën 2CV."

"Citroën 2CV!" Robert found himself laughing, and he moved closer to Alice. "Your Citroën 2CV was a blessing. It saved me from death and also made me meet you." Robert pressed his lips closer to Alice's

"My Citroën 2CV was a slow tortoise." She said, and then she craned her pouted mouth towards Robert's.

Soon, all that could be seen from the mountaintops were two parked Bentleys and two lovers teaching the world how to make love.

Alice and Robert never left that place again. The flower shop was abandoned, and Robert quit his job.

The rumor is going on that some of the most beautiful love story books being published the recent years where painted by their truly amazing love…..

STAY IN CONTACT WITH THE AUTHOR

mbolle@michel-bolle.com

http://www.michel-bolle.com

https://www.facebook.com/michel.bolle

www.ingramcontent.com/pod-product-compliance
Lightning Source LLC
LaVergne TN
LVHW041207150826
845673LV00001B/313

* 9 7 9 8 3 7 1 5 7 3 5 4 4 *